QUICKSILVER

QUICKSILVER

STEPHANIE SPINNER

Alfred A. Knopf

New York

THIS IS A BORZOI BOOK PUBLISHED BY ALFRED A. KNOPF

 Published in the United States of America by Alfred A. Knopf, an imprint of Random House Children's Books, a division of Random House, Inc., New York, and simultaneously in Canada by Random House of Canada Limited, Toronto. Distributed by Random House, Inc., New York.

www.randomhouse.com/teens

Library of Congress Cataloging-in-Publication Data
Spinner, Stephanie.
Quicksilver / Stephanie Spinner. — 1st ed.
p. cm.
SUMMARY: Hermes, Prince of Thieves and son of Zeus, relates why the seasons change, the history of the Trojan War, his friendship with Pegasus, and many more adventures.
ISBN 0-375-82638-6 (trade) — ISBN 0-375-92638-0 (lib. bdg.)
1. Hermes (Greek deity)—Juvenile fiction. [1. Hermes (Greek deity)—Fiction. 2. Mythology, Greek—Fiction.] I. Title.
PZ7.S7567Qs 2005
[Fic]—dc22
2004010311

Printed in the United States of America
April 2005
10 9 8 7 6 5 4 3 2 1
First Edition

for Tom Walker

CONTENTS

The world is full of Zeus' children, and I am one. If my infant antics had not attracted my father's attention, I might have lived out my days as a shepherd or a farm boy, thinking only of forage and livestock and weather. But on my first day of life I tricked my brother Apollo so thoroughly that he lost his composure in public. This unprecedented event made Zeus laugh for the first time in decades.

"You have a real talent for mischief," he told me as I stood before him in my swaddling clothes. "I can use someone like you."

So he made me his messenger.

PART ONE

Hell

ONE

It's dark and gloomy, and it smells like dead sheep, but when Zeus says go to Hell, I go. The Lord of All Creation is not a patient deity. Have you ever seen his hands clench and unclench when he's kept waiting? I call it the Thunderbolt Reflex. Best not trigger it is my advice, unless you long to burst into flame and explode.

I do not.

So today, when Zeus summoned me, I flew right over to his audience hall in my trusty winged sandals. I chose a very high speed—gazelle-fleeing-lion—and was there in a breath, ready with a good joke (the one about the mortal crossing the road) and a cheerful smile. Then I saw the scowl on Zeus' face and restrained myself. Joking with my father when he's testy is like challenging the Gorgons to a staring contest. Bad idea.

And the Master of the Universe was definitely fuming. Not only that, his sister Demeter was at his feet, sobbing. Her hair was undone, her robes were torn and gaping, and her upturned face was slick with tears. She had clawed at her exposed shoulders, raising crisscrosses of bleeding welts, like a mourner in the first throes of grief.

The sight sent a thrill of alarm through me. A thrill of curiosity, too: what had caused the Harvest Goddess such frenzied sorrow? She was normally the most placid of beings.

"Hermes!" growled Zeus. "Do you know what that brother of mine has done?"

I shook my head. Zeus could only be referring to Hades, Lord of the Underworld. His other brother, Poseidon, who was perfectly happy riding waves, watching whales, and chasing mermaids, took very little interest in mortal affairs, which was probably why his relations with Zeus were both distant and amicable.

So it must be Uncle Hades.

When I think of Hades, I feel as if I'm falling and shrinking at the same time. If this sounds unpleasant, it is, believe me. The god has no levity, no humor, and no charm. He's been a walking bad mood ever since the day Zeus and Poseidon got all the best parts of creation, leaving him with the Underworld, which, as I mentioned, is an armpit.

And—no surprise—Hades likes to share his misery. Like a bullying host who presses stale bread and sour wine on his guests, daring them to refuse, Hades makes it impossible for anyone in his purview to breathe freely or step lightly.

How? By devising something called The Underworld Codes and Regulations, a set of rules so impossible to remember, much less follow, that it makes Babylonian etiquette look easy.

Because of the Regulations, the instant you enter Hades' domain, you're doing something wrong—by looking left instead of right (Unlawful Beholding and Viewing, section 32, subsection 11), saying the wrong thing (Maladroit Utterance, sections 1–87), or touching something forbidden (Heinous Tactile Errors, part 560).

Your punishment? You're there forever. And if you've come from Brother Zeus' territory, so much the better. Hades hates Zeus.

The feeling is mutual.

"He's taken Kore," Zeus rumbled. Hearing her daughter's name, Demeter wailed and struck the floor with her forehead. She and Kore are very close. Zeus raised his voice over Demeter's keening. "Forced her to marry him," he called out.

Not much surprises me, but this did. Kore,

Demeter's only child, was a young wildflower of a girl—barefoot, meadow-dancing, and underdressed. She behaved more like a nymph than a goddess, and I couldn't for the life of me picture her in Hell. Neither, clearly, could Demeter.

"Bring her back, Zeus!" she screamed. "I can't live without her!" She resumed her sobbing, and her tears pooled at Zeus' feet.

He stepped away from her quickly, looking apprehensive. An unhappy goddess is never fun to be around, but Demeter's mood was downright ominous. In her way, she was as powerful as Zeus. Like him, she could do lots of damage.

I threw him a sympathetic look.

"She's stopped working," he said quietly.

"Really?" *There's bad news*, I thought. Without Demeter's attentions, crops on earth wouldn't grow, and livestock wouldn't breed. That meant drought, famine, pestilence, and a high mortal death rate—not to mention a sharp decline in offerings to us.

He nodded. "She's been cursing the harvests."

"And I'll keep cursing them," Demeter vowed, rising unsteadily and swiping at her bleary face with her gown, "unless you bring her back!"

What would Zeus do next? My prophetic gift kicks in sporadically, never on command, so I had to guess. Knowing Zeus' weakness for mortals (especially pretty ones), I reasoned that he'd want to prevent any disasters leading to their extinction, which meant placating Demeter.

Or did it?

If Zeus rescued Kore, he'd be provoking Hades, who could be a vicious adversary.

"Tricky situation," I ventured.

Zeus raised his big, bushy eyebrows in agreement.

Which is why you called me, I thought.

As usual, I was right.

TWO

I've been stealing since I was born. Really. When I was one day old, I hopped out of my cradle and stole fifty cows from Apollo—in my swaddling clothes, I might add. I almost got away with it, too, but Zeus made me confess. I didn't mind—I was only playing, and Apollo did forgive me right away. As for Zeus, the trick made him laugh long and hard, and he's had a soft spot for me ever since. Now I'm called Prince of Thieves, which I don't mind, either; I like my work.

Stealing isn't the only thing I do, of course. I escort the dead to the Underworld, carry messages for the Immortals, guide travelers, invent musical instruments, and protect animals. In my spare time I bring luck. I'm reasonably good at all these things, but when it comes to theft, I excel. No other god had the wherewithal to hustle down to Hell and steal back Hades' bride with a minimum of fuss, and Zeus knew it.

So, minutes after our conversation, I was in his chariot, happily taking up the reins. When Zeus told me I could drive it down to the Underworld, I nearly whooped for joy. His six colossal horses are as swift and powerful as his thunderbolts; they fairly rip through the sky. I'm no slowpoke, but they can run circles around me. Zeus had never let me near them—until today.

"I'll be careful, I promise" were my parting words.

Now, as I clucked them on, caution was the last thing on my mind. "How fast can you really go?" I whispered.

They heard me.

Their ears went flat and they leaped into the air like sparks out of a fire. *Holy Charybdis!* I thought, my stomach dropping. Mount Olympus fell away until its snowy peak was a white blur, and as we rose even higher, I clenched my eyes against the frigid blaze of starlight. I could swear I felt the crackle of ice in my lungs.

Then the horses dropped without warning, and we were tumbling through the heavens like lava coursing down Mount Etna.

It was supremely exciting. *If we crash, who cares?* I thought, giggling helplessly as we approached the earth. It was the best ride I'd ever had.

Then, as the hills of Arcadia rose up to meet us, the horses slowed, and their headlong plunge became a stately, measured canter. It wasn't my doing—I was so giddy I was barely hanging on to the reins—but by the time we got to the mouth of Taenarus Cave, they were trotting.

In we went, as smoothly as you please. I come here all the time—I lead the dead down to Hades through the cave—but Zeus' horses had never made the trip, so I was afraid they'd be skittish in the tunnel. But they weren't. They jogged along with perfect composure, and before long I'd regained my composure, too.

When I was finally breathing normally again, I began to compare the good and bad points of my situation. I had started doing this long ago, on the advice of my brother Apollo. He believes in taking stock, reasoning things out, and planning carefully. Of course I'd already agreed to rescue Kore. But I'd fallen into the habit of making lists in my head anyway, and now I did it just for fun.

Good

Incredible ride
Unforeseen, possibly thrilling dangers
Warm gratitude of lovely Kore (& her mother)
Rolling tide of rich mortal offerings
Paternal approval (always a plus)

Bad

Hades isn't called the Lord of Darkness for nothing; he holds a mean grudge

Well, that's clear enough, I thought. *The good far outweighs the bad*. That had been Zeus' view also.

"If Hades tries to stop you," he'd advised as I was leaving, "quote the Regulations to him. Kore's free to leave if she hasn't eaten anything. It's a footnote in the Admissions section."

The Regulations are endless and incredibly boring. I couldn't believe that Zeus had actually read them, but he can be surprisingly thorough sometimes. And he has an amazing memory.

"'Any being admitted to Hades,'" he'd recited, "'must remain for 46 million lunar cycles or in perpetuity, whichever is longer, if he, she, or it has consumed the Food of the Dead. If, while in Hades, said being has not chewed, swallowed, inhaled, absorbed, or in any other manner ingested the aforementioned Food of the Dead, he, she, or it may leave upon verbal or written request.'"

"How could she eat *anything* in that place?" Demeter had cried. "It's a sinkhole!"

"She probably hasn't," Zeus had replied, and I agreed. Kore is an Immortal; like the rest of us, she eats only for amusement. She wouldn't eat Down There—she'd be too miserable. And in that case, my job would be much easier. Old Stickler Hades had to abide by his own Regulations, didn't he?

THREE

There's no sun in Hell, only a grayish half-light like winter fog. The air is still, static as only a place without weather can be, and faintly acrid. The horses coughed with their first breath of it. I couldn't blame them. Though I've been here countless times, that first whiff always put me off, too.

I slowed the horses to a walk as we neared the river. The Styx isn't much more than a deep channel, but its milky green waters are poisonous, so I'd decided to leave the horses behind just to be safe. I told them to halt and they did.

"Hermes? Is that you?" Paddling toward us was old Charon, who ferries the dead across the river. His sight is bad, but his ears are as big as discuses, and very sharp.

I will sometimes startle him by approaching his ferry very, very quietly (which he hates), but not today. There was no sneaking up on him with six horses.

Charon is irascible and greedy. He demands—and gets—money from every one of his passengers, which to me is adding insult to injury. In my opinion it's bad enough to be dead without having to pay for transportation, too. And what can Charon possibly do with the money? There's not much to buy down here.

"Yes, it is," I replied, stepping down from the chariot carefully. The riverbank was muddy, and I wanted to keep my sandals clean. I would need speed today, and infernal mud tends to slow them.

"I thought so," he grunted. Across the river, Cerberus jumped and snarled, showing far too many teeth, even for a dog with three heads. I was glad, as I always am, that he was chained. Cerberus is Hell's watchdog. He stops escapees by eating them. With all three mouths going, it's a hideous sight.

I tied up the horses and checked my provisions: ox-liver treats for Cerberus, Cap of Invisibility for me, silver coin for Charon. Then I boarded the ferry.

After crossing the Styx, I skirted the Asphodel Fields, the place where most mortals go when they die. As always, the flat green expanses were splashed with white, pink, and yellow asphodels in bloom, and the air was milder and less acrid than it was at the river.

The fields are pleasant enough, in a spare, featureless way—nothing but flowers, a few shade trees, and the occasional cloth pavilion to break the monotony. Of course the dead don't really need much more: they don't eat, they don't sleep, and they don't need shelter because the weather's always mild. So they're left to wander listlessly, trading gossip and complaining about the lack of entertainment.

They're overjoyed to see me when I visit because I tell them jokes. And I have to admit they're my best audience. They like puns. They like riddles. They even like mortal jokes.

"What did the mortal say when Cerberus bit him? 'Ouch! Ouch! Ouch!'" makes them howl. And "What did Zeus say when the mortal built a house near Mount Olympus? 'There goes the neighborhood'" gets them every time.

I usually can't resist the temptation to make them laugh. But today I didn't stop. I was bound for the other part of Hell, where the wicked live in torment and Hades lives in a bad mood: Tartarus.

It was there that I would find Kore.

FOUR

Tartarus is near the fields, but so different it could be in another realm altogether. It's dank and stony, a soul-shredder of a place where the wicked suffer and the Furies come to watch. Whenever I visit, I feel as if I'm losing buoyancy; the wings on my sandals seem like weights, and moving swiftly takes effort.

I passed through the great obsidian portals of Hades' palace, whose gleaming black surfaces turn every visitor's reflection into a wraith, and got ready to see Tityus.

I am never quite prepared.

One step inside and there he was, poor giant, splayed on a stone platform, writhing against his chains as two enormous, blank-eyed vultures tore hungrily at his liver. It was his punishment—his eternal punishment—

for offending Zeus. Did I mention that my father could be harsh at times?

The three Furies watched from below, as gleeful as undetected felons at a public execution. This was how the bright-eyed, sharp-faced crones took a break from hounding and tormenting guilty mortals: they watched evisceration. I've seen them place bets on which vulture would make Tityus scream the loudest.

The grisly spectacle was Hades' way of saying hello.

I hurried along the stone passageway, trying as always to ignore Tityus' cries, and soon came upon a man flailing in the air above a food-laden banquet table. This was Tantalus, whose mad hubris had led him to kill his young son, cook him up, and feed him to Zeus and Demeter. He'd wanted to test them, to see if they knew what they were eating. Their horror quickly became implacable wrath, and they hung Tantalus here like a fly in a web, to starve for all time.

You were wrong about the gods, I thought, passing him by. *They do know everything. They just don't always pay attention.*

The last unfortunate in this dreary exhibit was Sisyphus. To me he was the saddest of all, though the others might disagree. If offered the choice, Tityus or Tantalus might actually prefer his punishment to their own, for Sisyphus was not suffering daily liver extraction or acute, aching starvation. He was merely pushing a huge boulder up a steep stone ramp only to see it roll down again, over and over and over until the end of time.

I paused for a moment at the base of the ramp. Sisyphus had once been a king famed for his cleverness. He had founded the great city of Corinth and then dared to capture Thanatos the Death Spirit so that no one on earth could die. This bold act had angered both Hades and Zeus to the frothing point, and in a rare moment of fraternal accord they had cast him down here. Now he knew only sweat and frustration.

It was a splendid trick, I thought, watching his slow ascent. *Inspired. If it were up to me, I'd free you right now.*

The moral support was unspoken and probably didn't help him one bit. But I couldn't do more, unless I was willing to face a thunderbolt or two, which I was not. So I pushed away my futile thoughts and summoned up a burst of speed.

It was time to face Hades.

FIVE

There are many long, immensely tall stone corridors on the way to the throne room, but my winged sandals made short work of them, even at old-man-chases-young-thief speed, which was the best I could do at the moment. When I arrived at the entry, the four blank-faced guards remained impassive, probably because they couldn't see me. An unseen arrival provides many opportunities for eavesdropping and borrowing, two of my favorite pastimes, so I was already wearing my Cap of Invisibility.

I glided in past the guards. Hades was on his black diamond throne, deep in conversation with Kore, who sat beside him on a gleaming new diamond throne of her own. She looked as beautiful as ever, slim and barefoot and slightly unkempt. But now she wore garlands of gold and gems rather than flowers, and a morose pout.

Except for the guards, she and Hades were alone.

"But why?" Hades was asking, almost pleadingly, as I drew near and settled down.

"Because it's ugly!" she replied, twining a long wheat-colored ringlet around her index finger. "Because a garden should be beautiful, and fragrant, and uplifting! It should have a . . . a soul, not a . . . what did you call it? A *projected* something?"

"Projected yield."

"Incredible," she murmured, shaking her head so that her curls rearranged themselves fetchingly on her bosom. She picked up another ringlet and teased it, unaware of the effect she was having on Hades, who watched her slack-mouthed.

He's practically drooling, I thought. *I've never seen him like this*. And then it came to me: Hades was in love.

My sour, nitpicky, rules-and-regulations uncle in love? What a wonderful joke! I stopped my laughter just in time by squeezing my nose and bending double. My eyes teared up with the effort.

"Give Ascalaphus a different job," said Kore.

"But he's an excellent gardener," objected Hades. "He works wonders down here, without any sunshine or rainfall! And he's not suited for much else. Not the sharpest sword in the armory, poor man."

She played with her hair in silence.

"His radishes are very tasty. His leeks, too. And those peaches of his are delicious. Just the sight of them drives Tantalus wild. You really should try one," he added, with a quick glance at her.

She exhaled derisively. "If you insist on keeping me here," she said, "I'd like *something* to do. Something I actually *enjoy*—like gardening."

"But—" Hades began.

"It's not as if I don't know how," she interrupted. "I've worked with my mother, Demeter—Goddess of the Cornfield, Barley Mistress, *Torch-Bearing Fury*"—she pronounced this with angry emphasis—"all my life. Before you kidnapped me, I was nurturing the crops of entire countries. If that means anything," she concluded bitterly.

Hades was visibly stricken. "I—I want you to be happy," he stammered.

"If you won't let me go, let me have the garden." She looked him in the eye without a trace of fear; at that moment she could have been her mother's twin.

Hades sighed. The lines in his face seemed to deepen. Then he bowed his head slowly, giving assent. "I'll speak to Ascalaphus," he said, rising. "Best if you stay here."

"As you wish," replied Kore, watching impassively as he strode away. The instant he was gone, her face softened, her eyes filled with tears, and she let out a high whimper, like a kitten's. Then, eyes clenched, she began to cry in earnest, wailing and sobbing much as Demeter had. It was a sorry sight.

I leaped to my feet, pulling off my cap. "Kore!" I said. "Don't cry."

Seeing me, she yelped in surprise. "Hermes! What are *you* doing here?"

"I've come to take you home," I said. "If you'd like to go." I smiled. "Would you?"

"Ha!" She laughed, choked, coughed, and finally recovered herself. "What do *you* think?" Before I could reply, she wiped her face on her skirt and leaped up to embrace me. She was slender but muscular, smelling of hay and chamomile. "It is *very* good to see you," she said. Her bare feet had landed on my toes, and now she drew away.

"Thanks," I replied, wishing I could put on my cap again. I was blushing furiously.

Kore took no notice. "How is my mother?" she asked.

"Very unhappy without you."

She blinked, eyes brimming. "I miss her so," she said. "Does she know where I am?"

I nodded. "She persuaded Zeus to send me here. I have his chariot," I told her, trying not to sound boastful. Still, I was pleased to see her eyes widen. Zeus' chariot was legendary. "I can fly you to Olympus as soon as you are ready," I said, "but first—"

"I'm ready now!" she cried, grasping my hand and hauling me toward the door so forcefully that I nearly tripped over my ankle wings. I enjoyed her strong grip almost as much as her embrace; even so, I managed to halt her in the corridor.

"You have to ask Hades' permission."

That stopped her. "He won't let me go."

"He must," I said, "by his own decree." And I quoted: "'Any being admitted to Hades must remain for 46 million lunar cycles or in perpetuity, whichever is longer, if he, she, or it has consumed the Food of the

Dead. If, while in Hades, said being has not chewed, swallowed, inhaled, absorbed, or in any other manner ingested the aforementioned Food of the Dead, he, she, or it may leave upon verbal or written request.'"

"Ah," said Kore.

Perhaps she doesn't understand, I thought, so I added, "As long as you haven't eaten anything, all you have to do is ask him to release you, and he'll have to do it. By the way, I hear the food down here is terrible."

"Mmm . . . the radishes look decent," she responded vaguely. I knew that tone of voice all too well; I used it often, when I couldn't tell the truth but didn't want to lie. Evasion is one of my standbys.

Then she asked, "Could I try on your cap? Maybe wear it until we get to the garden?"

"Why not?" I handed it to her and she put it on, then twirled before me in her bare feet. "Am I invisible?" she asked eagerly.

Her hopeful smile betrayed her.

"Sorry, Kore. It only works for me." This wasn't strictly true. I could command it to work for anyone, but I wasn't about to tell her so. I had to abide by Hades' Regulations; Zeus had been firm about that. Eyes downcast, she handed it back, and we walked on in silence.

Nice try, I thought, wondering what she'd eaten and knowing I'd find out all too soon.

SIX

Hades' garden is just an ordinary little kitchen patch—a few rows of vegetables and herbs, some fruit trees, and a grape arbor—sitting at the back of the palace. It was certainly nothing to get exercised about, at least in my opinion, but as Kore and I walked in, we could see that Ascalaphus, a tall, stooped man wearing a filthy apron and a knotted head rag, was very troubled indeed. The shovel in his hands looked as if it were just barely propping him up, and he was staring at Hades like a stunned sacrificial bull.

"Kore wants it?" he said. "But it's mine! I've tended it for centuries. I want to keep tending it."

"I've already told you, Ascalaphus," said Hades. "You deserve an easier job—something less demanding than the garden. And it doesn't have to be Sisyphus," he continued. "If you don't want to push his boulder down from the top of the ramp, you don't have to—though I thought you'd enjoy it."

Ascalaphus shook his head morosely.

"Maybe you could throw a grape at Tantalus every now and then," suggested Hades. "Add to his torment. What do you say?" Then, seeing us, he exclaimed, "Hermes! What brings you here?"

"Greetings, Uncle," I replied. "I've come at my father's behest."

"You usually do," he replied sourly. "And what does he want?"

"He wants you to let me go," Kore announced. "Hermes has come to take me home. I'm leaving, Hades."

"Leaving!" echoed Hades, looking even more dumbfounded than his gardener. "But I've just finished telling

Ascalaphus about the garden, that you wish to tend it."

Ascalaphus was glaring at Kore as if she were a weed he'd like to pull, but she failed to notice; she was intent on prompting me. "Tell him," she said. "Remind him about the rule."

"Rule? What rule?" asked Hades.

"It's in your Codes and Regulations," I said. "In section 46, subsection 2. And I quote: 'Any being admitted to Hades must remain for 46 million lunar cycles or in perpetuity, whichever is longer, and must thereinafter abide by all existing Codes and Regulations as well as those not yet formulated, particularly in regard to egress, which is strictly prohibited.'"

"Exactly," said Hades, with an I-rest-my-case glance at Kore, who prodded me nervously.

"There's a footnote to the section," I said. "It reads as follows: 'If, while in Hades, said being has not chewed, swallowed, inhaled, absorbed, or in any other manner ingested the Food of the Dead, he, she, or it may leave upon verbal or written request.'"

Hades took this reminder of his own handiwork stolidly, and when Kore quickly made her formal request, he granted it with a nod. But when she turned and began to hurry away without a goodbye, he watched with such profound sadness that I felt sorry for him.

Heartbroken, I thought, finding it not funny at all.

"She's going?" Ascalaphus was confused.

"I can't keep her. It's in the Regulations," said Hades.

He was still trying to explain his wife's departure—by now she was skipping into the palace—when I took my leave. With effort I pushed into dog-running-to-long-lost-master and caught up with her at Sisyphus' ramp. She was running hard, panting.

"You ate something, didn't you?" I said. We passed Sisyphus, who watched us from the corner of his eye but kept on climbing.

She slowed down. "I couldn't help it," she admitted. "I was bored, and the fruit looked so good. I ate five pomegranate seeds, that's all. But Hades didn't see me."

Let's hope not, I thought. We neared Tantalus, who was straining to reach a gleaming pitcher inches below him and failing. Grunts of desperation gave way to screams of frustration. The Furies, perhaps bored with Tityus, had settled near Tantalus like a trio of crows. They watched happily, gobbling fruit, cheese, and olives.

"Hermes, take me with you!" Tantalus shouted. "I'll reward you handsomely, I swear! Just cut me down!"

I have no sympathy for Tantalus. His crime was heinous, far worse than anything Sisyphus or Tityus ever did, yet he cries for mercy, while they suffer in silence. On the other hand, the Furies mock him with special savagery. I've seen them offer him bits of meat, calling it child's flesh, and then, when he reached for it anyway, drop it to the floor so he couldn't have it.

"Maybe next time," I called.

Zeus' team watched us with their ears pricked as we crossed back over the Styx on the raft. "There they are," I said proudly. "The fastest horses in creation. You'd better hang on to me when we take off."

"I will," breathed Kore.

I felt positively heroic.

SEVEN

The horses were eager to go. They danced in place, nodding their massive heads and swishing their tails. Kore stood behind me and wrapped her arms around my waist, her breath warm on my back as I took up the reins. It was a most pleasant sensation.

"Ready?" I asked.

"Stop!" The shout cut off her reply. It was Hades, who stood with Ascalaphus on Charon's ferry. "Stop," he repeated, "before I bring on the Furies!" They were mid-river. Charon was rowing harder than a galley slave in a sea battle.

Kore clutched me. "Let's go!" she whispered. "We can still get away!"

I turned to stare at her. No one gets away from the

Furies. If Hades sent them, they would follow us twice around the world, screeching lustily all the way, and Kore knew it. But if she knew, she didn't care, because she snatched the reins from me and cracked them, hard, before I could stop her.

Hades jumped onto the shore. "Kore!" he cried. It was the sound of raw torment, as pained as anything I had ever heard from Tityus, or Tantalus, or Sisyphus. Ascalaphus trailed him, bellowing.

And then two things happened: Ascalaphus charged at us, and the horses leaped into the air.

We were about six feet off the ground when Ascalaphus caught hold of a wheel. And then, like a bear clambering over a log, he hoisted himself into the chariot.

"I am coming with you," he grunted.

"Hermes!" gasped Kore, clutching my chest, but there was nothing I could do; the startled horses were bucking and rearing in the air, and it took all my strength to subdue them.

As I did, I wondered what had prompted Ascalaphus to join us. Surely he wasn't trying to escape—he was too attached to his garden. But if he was chasing Kore out of loyalty to Hades, he was making a serious mistake. *If you succeed in bringing her back*, I thought, *you'll lose your precious garden. You're no match for Kore*. I felt a twinge of sympathy for him. He wasn't a bad fellow, though he could have used better manners. As we flew over the Asphodel Fields, he ranted at Kore.

"You lied. You betrayed your husband. You broke his heart. I've told him you ate those seeds. I saw you. I will tell Zeus. He will send you back. And then you will be Hades' wife forever."

Kore trembled as his accusations hit her. "Shut up, you stinking dung beetle!" she retorted, but it had no effect. He kept berating her through the tunnel, in the dark, all the way to the mouth of Taenarus Cave.

Meanwhile, the inevitable lists were taking shape in my mind.

Good

Kore reunited with Demeter; grateful to me for rescue

Zeus' horses unharmed; possibly available again

Bad

Ascalaphus swearing that Kore broke the rules

Zeus honor-bound to return her to Hades

Demeter miserably unhappy

No paternal approval, no horses, no Kore

There was no getting around it: the bad far outweighed the good. Zeus would be disappointed, and I'd never drive his team again, much less enjoy Kore's favor.

Unless I came up with a solution.

EIGHT

Demeter and Kore embraced with the kind of ferocity that wins wrestling matches, sobbing as they rocked back and forth in each other's arms.

It was a touching sight and it went on for a long time, long enough for Ascalaphus to begin a slow advance toward Zeus' throne. With his dirt-encrusted hands and leathery feet, his ragged kerchief and sweat-stained apron, the gardener looked distinctly out of place up here, and my father threw me a questioning look. I raised an eyebrow, indicating that I would keep silent until Ascalaphus had spoken.

Which, once Kore and Demeter had retreated to a corner with their arms around each other, he proceeded to do.

"Almighty Zeus, Father of Heaven, Leader of the

Fates, hear me!" he began. "I am Ascalaphus, Hades' gardener, and I have a complaint."

"Yes?"

"That woman"—he pointed in Kore's direction with a gnarled finger—"has ill-treated my master. She lied to him. Then she left him!"

Zeus' expression was not exactly one of moral outrage. He was often guilty of the very same behavior. "She lied?" he asked mildly. "How?"

Kore burrowed deeper into her mother's bosom, and Demeter clutched her daughter even more tightly.

"She said she had not eaten while she was with us. But she did. She ate five pomegranate seeds out of my garden!"

"You saw her?"

The gardener nodded.

"He lies!" wailed Kore.

"No!" cried Demeter.

"Be sure you are telling the truth," Zeus said to the gardener, with more than a hint of menace.

"I am, I swear it!"

Knowing the dire import of Ascalaphus' vow, Zeus began to lose his equanimity. I knew the signs—a slight narrowing of the great dark eyes, a sudden flare of the nostrils, a tensing of the broad hands. If his fingers twitched (Thunderbolt Reflex), we were all in for trouble.

Our eyes met. He summoned me by lifting his chin and I hurried to his side, standing so that Ascalaphus could not see my face. Demeter and Kore, now coiled in a loose embrace, watched us intently. Fortunately they were out of earshot.

Nevertheless Zeus kept his voice down. "Did Hades send him?"

"He jumped onto the chariot!"

"You should have pushed him off."

What would that *have solved?* I wondered, but I knew better than to ask.

"Did she eat the seeds?"

There was no point in lying. "I'm sure of it," I said. "She really had no right to leave."

He scowled. "I can't send her back. Demeter would never forgive me."

"You don't want that," I said, and he rolled his eyes in agreement. "I wonder if they'd compromise," I added, as if I'd just thought of it.

"Hades and Demeter?" He looked skeptical, and with good reason. Gods don't compromise; they consider it demeaning. Gods say what they want and get it, and if they don't, they do terrible, vengeful things. But this was an unusual situation, and it required an unusual resolution. "What do you have in mind, son?" he asked.

I loved it when he called me that, as if I were unique, not one of thousands.

"Say that Kore has to stay with Hades half the year because she ate the pomegranate seeds but that she can spend the rest of the year with Demeter."

His face brightened. "Clever!"

I maintained an air of modesty, though I agreed with him. It *was* a clever solution, and I knew it. "Thank you," I said, imagining myself vaulting into the blue behind his magnificent horses, with Kore at my side.

He patted my shoulder. "Let's hope it works."

Well, it did work, in a mixed-blessing kind of way. Since that time, mortals have had to put up with winter while Kore is with Hades, but they forget their woes as soon as she rejoins Demeter. The instant the two of them get together, the air warms, the earth turns fragrant, and green shoots start poking up out of the ground. The change makes mortals positively ecstatic. Since it began, they've become more generous—and more punctual—with their offerings.

Hades is happier now, too. I heard a rumor that he almost smiled once.

As for Father, he's been very generous with his horses. "Go! Enjoy!" he says when I ask to borrow them. I've taken them out dozens of times.

But Kore (who's taken to calling herself Persephone, now that she's married) won't come along. "I can't," she always says. "I'm just too busy. I don't know how Hades ever ran this place by himself!" Then, with a shake of her head, she rejoins her dryad assistants. She's got a dozen of them.

I was beginning to fear that marriage—and ruling the Underworld with her husband—had changed more than Kore's name, but I didn't want to believe it, so I kept trying to entice her away.

I made another attempt in late winter, on one of those

sweet, sunny days that cry out for celebration. I found Kore sitting near the garden (which now included beds of tall, solemn black flowers), surrounded by her dryads. Every time she spoke, they nodded. When I landed the chariot, they stared, then turned back to their conversation.

"Care for a ride?" I called, trying to sound offhand.

Kore looked at me. Her hair was bound up in the manner of a young matron, and her gown was rich and severe, a garment of deadly respectability. "I really can't," she said. I cringed; her voice rang with the insincere regret of an adult denying a child.

I never asked again.

PART TWO

Medusa's Cave

NINE

After I rescued Kore, Zeus took to calling me "Head Psychopomp." It was a silly title—there's only one psychopomp, or guide for the dead, on Mount Olympus, and that's me. But the way he said it made me feel important and mysterious, so I never dreamed of objecting. I did dream of going on another mission, however, just to break the routine of my trips to Hell.

So when Zeus summoned me to his audience room one golden summer afternoon, I tied on my sandals and flew over at hawk-chases-sparrow, one of my faster speeds.

I was eager to hear why he needed me.

Zeus, however, took his time getting to the point. Perseus, a young prince, was seeking his help. Like many young mortals, he was Zeus' son, and this gave him an advantage. Zeus liked to help his offspring.

"I suppose you know he's mine," he said.

I nodded. We were sharing a tot of ambrosia while Helios, the Sun God, drove his chariot west. It sank below the horizon, and the sky sang a raucous hymn to red, purple, and gold.

"He's turned out rather well, considering," Zeus murmured.

Considering the grief you caused his mother, Danae? I thought. *Yes, he has.* Danae's troubles began when her father, King Acrisius, heard a prophecy that his yet-unborn grandson would kill him. Foolishly hoping to outwit the Fates, he locked Danae in a bronze chamber, where no man could reach her.

No man did.

Zeus was another story.

Ever resourceful when it came to lissome mortal girls, he changed himself into a shower of gold, poured in through Danae's window, and seduced her.

When Perseus was born, Acrisius feared for his life more than ever, so he locked Danae and the baby into a wooden box and put them out to sea. Eventually they washed up on the island of Seriphos, where they were taken in by Dictys, a good-hearted fisherman whose brother Polydectes ruled the island.

"I look in on them sometimes," Zeus confessed in a whisper. His wife, Hera, might be near, and her jealousy was volcanic. "Perseus has grown into a fine boy. He's been trying to fend off Polydectes for more than a year." The king was infatuated with Danae and kept proposing marriage. She kept refusing. After plying her with sweet words, a heifer, and olives from the mainland, he had resorted to threats.

Perseus was young, strong, and fearless. He told Polydectes defiantly that Danae would not be coerced into marriage. Polydectes had no desire to fight Perseus man-to-man, so he lied, saying he'd decided to marry another woman.

"All my courtiers," he added, "are giving me fine horses as wedding gifts. You will do that, too, I trust?" He said this knowing how poor the boy was, and how proud.

Perseus fell into the trap. "I cannot give you horses," he said, "but will give you any other gift you wish."

"Then bring me the head of Gorgon Medusa," retorted the king.

Medusa, with her snaky hair, poisonous talons, and lethal glare, lived in a cave in Arcadia. She did not welcome visitors, so this was like telling Perseus to go kill himself. Fully aware that the king had tricked him, Perseus accepted the challenge without a blink. Then he went home to tell his mother, and she fainted.

"Polydectes is a swine," said Zeus.

I agreed.

"And you're not too busy right now, are you?"

I shook my head. I did not need my gift of prophecy to know what was coming.

"Good. He needs the Adamantine Sickle."

"Ares has it."

"Just take it."

Easy for you to say, I thought. I may be the Prince of Thieves, but Ares, God of War, is three times my size and as touchy as a caged badger, especially in peacetime. As far as I knew, the world was at peace today, so Ares would need delicate handling. But I was foolishly eager for the adventure, so all I said was, "Fine. Anything else?"

Zeus put his hand on my shoulder. "Can you spare your sandals? They would help Perseus a lot." My winged sandals are my dearest possession. I value them even more than my Cap of Invisibility or Caduceus, my spell-casting wand. My father knew this, of course.

I nodded and he patted me. As always, his approving

touch warmed my skin and quickened my heart, so that all I wanted to do was please him.

No wonder you have so many children, I thought. *You're irresistible*.

"And keep the boy out of trouble till he finishes the job, won't you? Make sure he gets back to his mother safely?" Again his voice dropped to a whisper. "Danae—"

He still had a soft spot for her. He was like that. "I know," I broke in. "She worries about him. Well, he's perfectly safe with me," I said, draining my goblet.

I believed it when I said it.

Ares' weapons room is as scrupulously clean as a shrine to Hestia, Goddess of the Hearth. All its contents are in perfect working order, which is more than I can say for the God of War himself. He's loud, messy, red-eyed, and restless, and when he's not fuming over some imagined slight, he's shouting or cursing. When he takes offense—

which is often—he bristles like a porcupine and the dark, wiry hair on his shoulders stands straight up. I have seen this. It is a repulsive sight.

Nobody likes him, least of all me, and I confess that when I rapped on the armory's tall bronze door, I was hoping he wouldn't be there. Ares wouldn't dare disobey Zeus' request for the sickle, but he'd be sure to give me a hard time before handing it over.

I knocked again and there was no response. *Lucky me*, I thought, opening the door. I'd take the sickle and Zeus would tell Ares why—easier all around.

I stepped inside.

The armory was as I remembered it, a serene place lined floor to ceiling with countless tools of war. Helmets—plumed, gilded, studded, skull-topped. Sheathed swords. Two-headed axes. Towering stacks of metal greaves and breastplates. Cuirasses of cloth, hide, and reptile skin, wrinkled and stained with battle sweat.

Poisonous decoctions. Massive gold and silver shields, some adorned with grinning shrunken heads. Throwing lances and thrusting lances, all tall as men. And, on its very own gilded stand in the center of the room, like a menacing, razor-sharp smile, the Adamantine Sickle.

Hephaestus, Fire God and master artisan, had made it long ago, forging it in secret out of nobody knew what. He called it Unconquerable, and after he demonstrated how it could slice an airborne flower petal, cut three sheaves of wheat with one stroke, and behead a snake as quietly as a whisper, everyone agreed it was a fitting name. When Ares saw the sickle, he wanted nothing else, and after days of haggling, pleading, angry demands, and lavish bribes, he finally got Hephaestus to sell it.

The price was so high that Ares wouldn't reveal it.

I do not like weapons, even when they are as beautiful as the sickle. This is very ungodlike; all the Olympians bear arms. Ares has his arsenal, Apollo and

Artemis their bows, Zeus his thunderbolts. Athena likes to be called the Goddess of Wisdom, but she is never without helmet, aegis, and armor. Even Love Goddess Aphrodite has a little golden dagger tucked into her magic girdle (don't ask me how I know).

I have always thought this ridiculous. Why should we Immortals carry weapons? Nothing can kill us. Nevertheless, the habit persists. Of all the gods, I alone rely on my wits for protection. It has always been a point of pride with me. Having said this, I'll confess that when I lifted the sickle off its stand, I fully understood why Ares had craved it so. The thing was as light and supple as a willow switch, falling into the crook of my arm as if it longed to be there. My *new death-dealing friend*, I thought. It made me feel utterly invincible, as cool and implacable as its silver moon blade.

I will not lie. I liked the feeling.

TEN

Arcadia is an easy trip from Olympus, due south over Thessaly and the Gulf of Corinth. Even carrying the sickle, I got there quickly—the day was clear, the winds were helpful, and my spirits were high. Apollo had given me excellent directions to Medusa's cave—he's good at that—so I found it easily.

I first saw Perseus from the air. He was sitting cross-legged on the ground beside Athena's great shield, lobbing pebbles into a hollow tree trunk some twenty paces away. His aim was good.

So were his reflexes. Coming down, I placed the sickle against a tree. It touched a branch, a leaf rustled, and he was on his feet, sword in hand. He looked around warily and I thought, *He's quick. Excellent.*

I took off my cap so that he could see me. "Perseus," I said in greeting.

"Hermes!" He was sixteen or so, nearly full-grown, with a boy's tremulous voice and a smooth, fine-boned face. Except for the white-gold braid that hung down his back, his pale hair was clipped to the skull. At first glance he looked more like a shepherd than a king's grandson—his hands were rough and his garment was country-spun. But his manners were good. He dropped his sword and fell to his knees instantly, bowing his head.

"Rise," I said, and he sprang to his feet with the awkward grace of a fawn rising out of a nest. "Let's plan our battle."

"You're coming? The goddess didn't tell me!" Surprise and pleasure transformed his face. Smiling, he was handsome.

"At least she remembered to give you her shield," I

said. Athena's memory is terrible—except for grudges. Hearing of Perseus' mission to kill Medusa, she had quickly volunteered her favorite weapon. The shield, polished to a mirror shine, lay on the forest floor, giving us a bright blue oval of sky. "She told you how to use it, I hope?"

He shook his head. "I know I can't look at Medusa, or I'll turn to stone like them." He pointed to a spot through the trees, about a hundred paces away, where a motionless parade of Medusa's victims approached the cave entrance. They looked startled, incredulous that her stare was lethal, even as it killed them.

"Poor fools," I said.

I backed away from Perseus. "I'll be Medusa. Come at me, but look at my reflection in the shield." I scowled hideously, wiggling my fingers around my head as if they were snakes. He forced a smile, but we both knew that battling the real Medusa would be no laughing matter.

She, who had once been a pretty young girl with beautiful dark ringlets, had remarked that her hair was lovelier than Athena's, and the silly boast had ruined her.

Hearing it, Athena had turned her into a monster, with live snakes for tresses. Grotesque and miserable, Medusa had retreated to a cave deep in Arcadia. Whatever kinship she had felt with mortals had long since turned to searing hatred. Those who found her found death also: her stare was so frightening that it turned mortal onlookers to stone.

Have I mentioned that the gods can be spiteful?

Now Perseus hoisted the shield with his left hand, grasping his sword with his right. Looking into the shield as if it were a mirror, he came toward me sideways, sword raised.

I hissed as Medusa might, slipping beyond his reach. He lunged at me again, and again I evaded him. He took a deep breath, preparing for another try. To his credit, he kept his dark blue eyes on the shield. This time I screeched and pretended to claw at his shoulder. He would have struck me if I hadn't used my winged sandals to leap high out of range.

"You have the right idea but the wrong tools," I told him. "Your sword is too short for the job."

"It's all I have," he said, without a hint of self-pity. I liked that.

The Adamantine Sickle was propped against one of the stone bodies near the cave. I retrieved it.

"Here," I said, offering it. "Try this."

He took it and his watchful, rather serious expression went from interest to downright wonder. He looked as blissful as if he'd just received one of Aphrodite's warmest smiles.

"Better than your sword, don't you think?"

He hefted it. "Much better," he said slowly. Then, without warning, he took a quick swing at me that I just barely managed to avoid. When I ducked, he actually laughed.

I was amazed by his lack of respect. I might look his age, but I was ageless and divine; he knew that. "Careful!" I snapped. "You won't last long in there if you act like a buffoon."

At my rebuke I saw his hand tighten around the weapon's shaft possessively. *It's the sickle*, I thought, *bewitching him!* Remembering how the weapon's mere touch had made me giddy, I realized that it could do much worse to Perseus. He, being mortal, lacked the strength of mind that comes with divinity. What if it made him mad? Zeus would never forgive me.

"Don't get too attached to that thing," I said sharply. "It belongs to Ares. He'll want it back." *There's an understatement*, I thought.

"I won't." He sounded sincere. But I resolved to watch him very closely.

ELEVEN

Perseus set to practicing, and Athena's shield became an oval flame, flickering in the noonday sun. I watched him for signs of mental imbalance, but if the sickle was doing anything, it seemed to be boosting his strength and skill. Before long he was handling both weapons with ease.

Meanwhile, Medusa was curled up in a cool, dark corner of her cave, asleep against the afternoon heat. Athena, who took a fitful, vengeful interest in Medusa's habits, had told me this herself, saying it would be the perfect time to attack. I decided to follow her advice.

"Perseus!" I beckoned. "Let's go in." I held out my winged sandals. "Put these on. They'll help you, too." Stammering thanks, he laid down the sickle and knelt to tie on the sandals.

A wicked impulse seized me. I grabbed the sickle and swung it over his head, close enough to cut his short hair even shorter. He yelped, clutching at his pate, which now boasted a large, angry pink bald spot.

"Oh, sorry," I said, not sorry at all. "Didn't mean to hit you."

He rubbed his head, looking stricken. *That will teach you to be rude to an Immortal*, I thought. Then I softened. I am not a grudge-bearing god. "Stand up and try them," I said, indicating the sandals.

He hastened to obey. After lacing them up quickly, he took a few short steps in my direction. They lifted him a hand's breadth above the ground and his face went slack with delight.

"Jump," I said, and he did, whooping like a loon when he shot into the air.

"Quiet!" I waved him down. "She's asleep! Now keep silent and practice with everything—the shield, the sickle, and the sandals." As I handed back the sickle, I had a lovely burst of inspiration. "By the way," I said, "you should know that the sickle was made for the gods. Its touch is slow poison to mortals." It was one of my better lies, and he blanched.

"You . . . you didn't tell me that before."

"Slipped my mind." I shrugged.

"What about the sandals?" He couldn't hide the alarm in his voice.

"They won't hurt you. But the sickle . . ." I shook my head warningly. It worked; he took hold of the thing as warily as if it were an angry viper, all traces of possessiveness gone.

"Now show me what you can do," I said. "And hurry. We should attack while she's napping. I hear she's especially nasty when she wakes."

As we walked to the cave a few minutes later, I said,

"Don't look at her face even after she's dead. It will still have the power to kill."

"Athena told me that," Perseus replied, averting his eyes from the hapless creatures Medusa had already turned to stone. There were many: men drawing swords, nocking bows, and brandishing spears; a cluster of ragged children; a pack of dogs, caught in mid-snarl; two ancient women carrying market baskets; and a trio of buzzards. All were rain-streaked. Some were mossy, which gave them the look of neglected temple statuary. It was a chilling display.

Inside the cave the air was cool and foul-smelling, the floor littered with bones. As Perseus and I picked our way through them, I wondered about Medusa's diet. From the size of the bones, she was eating mice, rats, and the occasional rabbit. But what about her hair? Did the snakes eat, too? And if so, did Medusa feed them? What a repugnant task that would be! The gloom of the place seemed to encourage such grisly speculation.

Or perhaps I was nervous. Perseus was in mortal danger, and I was accountable for his safety. That meant I had to stay safe also. Medusa's glance couldn't kill me, of course, but it might make me sick, according to Athena. She claimed that looking at Medusa gave her a splitting headache.

A loud, rasping sound, like a big, rusty saw plying an unwilling tree, came from a raised ledge about forty paces away. Medusa was snoring.

I gestured to Perseus to look only at the shield. He gave me a quick, tense nod and we drew closer. I had resolved to keep my eyes down, but when at last I could see Medusa in the darkness, my resolve left me, and I gaped.

TWELVE

She was a mongrel monster—a sorry jumble of human, serpent, and beast. Her body was covered with large, irregular dark scales. Her legs were muscular and furry, the paws ending in talons as big as grappling hooks. Another talon marked the end of her long, scaly serpent's tail.

And then there was her head.

Here Athena had been especially cruel. The goddess had stripped away Medusa's gleaming curls, replacing them with a nightmarish snarl of writhing mud-brown snakes. Yet she had left the girl's face intact. It was youthful and fresh-skinned, a perfect pale oval, and the snakes that surrounded it mocked its beauty.

Gone the admiring glances, they hissed. *Gone the beseeching love words, the paeans. Gone the many deep joys of self-regard. Now you belong to us.*

Seeing Medusa, I thought of the time when Zeus had sent me to kill Argos, the hundred-eyed monster. Argos never slept. When he grew drowsy, some of his eyes closed, but there were always others that stayed open and alert. I could not approach him unseen (it was before I had my Cap of Invisibility or Caduceus), so instead I charmed him with my flute, playing tune after tune of such beguiling sweetness that every single one of his hundred eyes finally dropped shut. Then I cut off his head.

Argos knew that when he succumbed to sleep, I would kill him; I had seen it in his pleading eyes. Yet I played on, watching them close slowly, helplessly. I could have put down my flute, sparing him for his love of music, but I did not. And now, suddenly, I felt a tremor of long-buried shame. It surprised me. Immortals never question their actions, I least of all. Yet there it was: I had killed a magnificent creature despite my compassion for it, and I was sorry.

Medusa stirred; her snoring stopped. Jolted, Perseus sprang forward, shield flashing, sickle whining. The sound threw the snakes into a frenzy of alarm, and their terrified flailing disturbed Medusa's sleep. As the blade came at her, she woke.

Her eyes opened and I met her death stare—recognition and grief mingled with pure, searing hatred. It was like being smothered in stinging nettles—pain so acute, so overwhelming, that it made time stop.

Her eyes widened, filling with blood. "You gods!" she groaned. Her head came away from her body and hit the ground, rolling until it stopped facedown at my feet. I stifled a whimper: the snakes still moved. Meanwhile, dark blood, oily and viscous, spurted from her headless neck.

As I stared at her lifeless body, my revulsion became sorrow—heavy, dark, guilt-laden. I hadn't killed Medusa, but I had made her death possible. *This is hateful,* I thought. *I'll never do it again.* With the vow my spirits lifted.

Perseus, meanwhile, had collapsed onto a ledge and lay there breathing heavily. As the pungent, metallic smell of Medusa's blood tinged the air, I reminded him not to look at her face when he picked up her head. He closed his eyes by way of reply.

But when he roused himself, his handling of the snakes was deft. They coiled and twined around his wrists, hissing in protest as he struggled to pack the head away with his eyes averted, yet he managed to maneuver it into the pouch Athena had given him without hurting them or himself. This done, he took up the shield and hurried outside. I picked up the sickle, which he had prudently left for me, and followed.

We blinked against the sunshine, breathing deeply. After the cave, the air tasted like ambrosia.

"You did well," I told Perseus. "It was a difficult task." This was an understatement, and we both knew it, yet he replied humbly, thanking me for my help.

"No need," I said. "I am here at Zeus' behest. But whatever you do," I added, "don't forget to offer to Athena. You may have noticed that she doesn't respond well to slights."

"I will make many rich offerings to her when I return to Seriphos," he said earnestly.

How long would that take? I wondered. Medusa's dying face came back to me, and I was seized with the desire to leave this place. I could take my winged sandals and go, I thought, leaving Perseus to return home on his own. Tempted, I began to weigh the pros and cons.

Leave

Perseus came here alone; he can return alone

Medusa's head will protect him

If Ares doesn't get his sickle back soon,

he'll blame me, not Zeus

Don't Leave

Nobody breaks a promise to Zeus

If Perseus is harmed, thunderbolts will fly

Singed hair and eyebrows are very unattractive

Before I got any further, a loud, wet, rustling sound came from the cave, as if a shipwrecked object were being hauled up out of the deep. Perseus and I looked at each other, startled.

"What—?" Before he could finish, we heard the unmistakable three-beat clop of a horse's hooves.

Hoofbeats? I thought. *Cantering? Impossible.*

A magnificent white horse burst out of the cave. It was as muscular as a Titan, with a pumping chest and long, powerful legs, but most dazzling were its wings. They flared wide and bright as the sails on a royal barge. Seeing us, the horse pinned its ears back and reared up on silver hooves. Then it gathered itself on its haunches and leaped into the air, wings beating with a deep luffing sound.

No! I thought with a stab of yearning. *Don't go!* I had no idea how the creature had arrived in the cave or where it was going—all I knew was that I couldn't bear to see it leave.

"Give me my sandals. Hurry!" I urged Perseus. I pulled off the left one while he undid the right and slapped them on without even doing up the laces. "Wait for me here," I called over my shoulder. Then I flew after the horse.

THIRTEEN

He was swifter than Zeus' team. Even when I pushed my sandals to their top speed—north-winds-gusting-in-winter—I couldn't catch him. I knew it long before I had chased him as far south as the skies above Libya. When I finally slowed to a jog and he went from a gallop to a lazy trot, we were still more than a hundred paces apart; in all this time I had not been able to get any closer.

I took a few deep breaths. He looked back at me, ears pricked. For a moment, neither of us moved.

Then, seeing the long curl of a river below, I decided to try a different approach. I left him in the clouds and flew down to earth, to the water's edge. As cranes strutted near the banks of the great brown river, I quickly fashioned a pipe out of reeds and played a few trills. It wasn't my best work, but it would do.

I returned to the sky. The horse was on the cloud bank where I had left him, ambling along with his wings at rest, but when he saw me, his plum-colored eyes rolled and he tensed for flight.

I had no intention of making him run. Instead, I stood with my back to him and began to play.

I started with a song about oats and apples and honeycombs and went right into one about rolling in soft, wet grass. After that I played a lullaby about warm flanks touching in the moonlight.

It wasn't until a second lullaby, about long tails swish, swish, swishing back and forth, that I dared to turn. I was pleased to see that his head drooped, his eyes were shut, and his great wings were folded. I rose, continuing to play, drawing ever closer. It was an excellent lullaby, very long. I played it twice.

Finally—and now I switched to something livelier,

about birdsong at dawn—I was on his back. He woke and his head shot up, but I was already soothing him, stroking his pulsing neck and whispering in his ear, calling him Pegasus, Moon-Hoofed, horse of my dreams.

His ears flicked and his tail swished; otherwise he was quiet. When I asked him to carry me back to Perseus, he obeyed as if he'd been mine forever.

I do not crave attention, like some Immortals I could mention, but I must admit that I enjoyed the look on Perseus' face as we came down before him.

"You . . . you caught him!"

I nodded with just a hint of godlike superiority and tossed him my sandals. "Now we both have wings," I said. "Are you ready to go home?"

FOURTEEN

It should have been a short trip, but it wasn't, because of the naked girl. Her name was Andromeda, and she was chained to a rock in the ocean, off the coast of Joppa. The very moment Perseus saw her, he fell for her. I mean that. One moment we were flying along companionably above the Sea of Cyrene. The next, he gasped loudly and went into free fall, plummeting like a winged duck. To my relief he soon recovered and was on his feet by the time he landed.

Then, with his eyes downcast (good manners again), he struck off the girl's chains with his sword and wrapped her in his cloak.

I watched this from above with a flush of pride. *Intrepid!* I thought. *Daring!* His time with me had clearly been good for him.

As for the girl, she must have been in some dream state far beyond terror, for she showed little emotion when Perseus freed her. Though she was soaked and shaking with cold and had just been saved from certain death, she thanked him with a nod and a smile, as if she were a princess on a receiving line.

As it happened, she *was* a princess, the only daughter of King Cepheus and Queen Cassiope of Joppa. They watched from shore, showing a lot more surprise than their daughter when Perseus dropped from the sky.

I could not hear Perseus and Andromeda, but I could see him take her hand in his and his blond head incline toward her dark one as they spoke, just as I could see the royal party and the sea serpent rearing up out of the choppy water like a cobra rising out of a basket, surprising everyone, including Pegasus, who behaved just like a horse and bolted.

He ran me halfway to Gallia before I could subdue

him, so I missed a lot. By the time I got him under control and turned him around, I was very worried, and I stayed worried all the way back to Joppa, telling myself I should have been there to help Perseus with the serpent, no matter what. If he'd failed to kill it, he'd be humiliated. If he'd been hurt (or worse!) in trying, I'd soon be dodging thunderbolts.

But when we got back to the seashore, the serpent was dead, lying headless in the shallows. A few bold children were climbing it and shrieking happily; otherwise the beach was deserted.

I guessed the royal party would be at the palace, so that's where I headed, keeping my eye out for signs of disaster. Seeing that the land below was dotted with sheep and goats, not mourners or funeral pyres, I neared the palace reasonably sure that Perseus was safe. After I'd wedged the sickle into the topmost branches of a tall oak and left Pegasus with a dumbstruck shepherd boy, I went inside.

I slipped in wearing my cap. Even if I'd remained visible, I might have escaped notice in the great hall—an extremely noisy banquet was in progress, with the king and queen presiding over a crowd of tipsy guests. Wine flowed like a river in spate, and the hall rang with shouts and jests, making it impossible to hear much, least of all the frail blind singer who stood in a corner at the rear of the hall, chanting an ode to Hymenaeus, the Marriage God.

Nevertheless, Andromeda was listening to the man with great interest, and so was Perseus. I stared at my charge in disbelief. *I leave you alone for a few minutes and you get married?* I thought incredulously.

The answer turned out to be yes.

FIFTEEN

I learned that the ceremony—performed in haste, in the courtyard—had just taken place. I also learned that Queen Cassiope was responsible for the sea serpent.

"We were strolling on the beach after the storm last week," one lady of the court informed another after they'd clinked wine goblets. "She told me she'd seen some Nereids and wasn't impressed. 'They're grotesque, Amenia!' she said. She didn't even lower her voice! That did it."

"What did what?" asked her companion.

"They heard her."

"No!" This was said with mock horror and genuine delight, and I wondered if everyone in the room disliked the queen as much as these two did.

The woman called Amenia rolled her eyes. "Carpa, you know how vain they are," she said. "They must have gone straight to Poseidon."

You're probably right, I thought. Nereids are sea nymphs, odd, beautiful creatures with silky fins on their backs and long, rainbow-hued limbs, who spend most of their time lolling in the ocean like seals. They appear affable, but they can be as touchy as goddesses. I think they're spoiled from all the tribute they receive. Nobody ever offers much to the river-and-stream nymphs, but Nereids get hefty sacrifices all the time because the oceans are so perilous. It's made them arrogant.

"After all," noted Amenia, "the serpent came the very next day." She and her friend then compared notes about its activities. Apparently it had eaten every fish within miles, drowned scores of luckless fishermen, and chewed up many fine vessels in the harbor, including one belonging to Carpa's husband. "Terrible loss to us, not that *she* cares," she said, indicating the queen.

Amenia leaned closer to Carpa. "Do you know what she said when the oracle told them to appease Poseidon by sacrificing Andromeda to the serpent?"

Carpa shook her head, rapt.

"She said, 'We can't sacrifice her! She's got to marry Agenor! That match is worth a fortune to us!'"

"No!"

Hearing this, I was a little shocked, too. *Not exactly a loving mother*, I thought.

Despite her objections, King Cepheus had gone ahead with the sacrifice, and the princess was duly chained to her rock. Perseus had appeared only moments later.

As for him, he demanded—and got—the promise of Andromeda's hand in return for killing the serpent. Now, listening respectfully to the singer's ancient ode, he seemed weary but happy. Andromeda, resplendent in a gold-trimmed gown, was no longer the dazed, distant girl I had seen earlier but bright-eyed and vividly beautiful. She held on to Perseus' arm as if she would never let it go.

He has certainly put in a full day, I thought, seeing him try to conceal a yawn. When the ode finally ended, he and Andromeda stood. They thanked the singer, who told them his name was Molpus. After Perseus poured him some wine—which he sniffed, pronounced excellent, and drank eagerly—the young couple started toward the front of the hall.

They were not far from the king and queen when shouts came from the other side of the room. Someone cried, "I won't stand for it! She's mine!" and there were angry sounds of assent, the kind men make when they work themselves up before battle.

All the joy left Andromeda's face.

"No stranger can take her!" Again the voice rose above the din. "She was promised to me!"

Andromeda moved closer to Perseus and whispered to him. His face tensed. He looked far less boyish than he had only a few hours ago, when I'd first met him. *Well, why not*, I thought. *He's certainly been doing a man's work.*

Perseus stepped in front of her, hand on his sword. When he was in the clear—many guests moved away, smelling trouble—I could see the makeshift strap slung across his chest and the leather pouch tied to it. Inside was Medusa's head.

Shoving Molpus aside, a tall, heavy-jawed man strode up to Perseus. "I am Agenor," he announced, chest heaving. "Andromeda is mine. We are betrothed."

He was roughly twice Perseus' size. The men with him—half a dozen glowering drunks—were not exactly dainty, either.

"You were her betrothed?" Perseus asked mildly. "Do you love her?"

Agenor sneered in confusion, as if he had never heard the words *love* and *betrothal* in the same sentence before. "Of course," he replied dismissively.

"Not enough to save my life," Andromeda pointed out.

True, I thought.

There were a few sympathetic murmurs from the guests, and somebody slurred, "Coward." A woman giggled. In the ensuing silence the air thickened with dire possibilities.

Then the queen called out, "Our promise to Perseus means nothing! He forced us into it." She lifted her chin at Agenor, prompting him, and he reached out for Andromeda. She recoiled; once again Perseus shielded her.

"You heard the queen," said Agenor.

Perseus kept silent, and his face was impassive, but I could swear he was thinking of his own mother, Danae. She too was a queen, but how unlike Cassiope! She disliked Polydectes and didn't want to marry him, yet she'd begged her son not to go after Medusa's head. His safety meant more to her than her own happiness.

And here was Andromeda's mother, casually discarding her daughter for the second time that day.

Perseus drew his sword.

Agenor struck at him and he parried. Then Perseus went on the attack, beating the larger man back and drawing blood with his third quick stroke. Agenor screamed, rage and surprise purpling his face. Seeing him bleed, his cohorts scattered.

I had been poised to intervene, but Perseus was holding his own perfectly well, and Agenor, clutching his wounded arm, looked as if he were reconsidering his claim on the princess.

Then, after a quick exchange with the queen, King Cepheus stepped in.

SIXTEEN

The king leaped to his feet, braying, "Perseus must die!" Perhaps thinking that her husband's statement needed clarification, Cassiope shrilled, "Kill him!"

A good many guests were too drunk to fight. They contented themselves with mumbling and staring and shifting in their seats. But a few energetic revelers managed to swarm Perseus and wrest his sword away. Ignoring Andromeda's horrified screams, Agenor jumped in for the kill.

It was time for me to reveal myself. I was just about to doff the Cap of Invisibility when I saw Perseus say something to Andromeda. She covered her eyes, Perseus pulled out Medusa's head, and Agenor saw it.

The man didn't even have time to blink. Hardening into stone as if the Gorgon's glare had blasted and baked him, he toppled with his sword upraised. The echoing crash of his fall drew everyone's attention.

Then came a long, eerie moment. It began with screams and shouts when Agenor shattered; continued as Perseus turned slowly in place, displaying Medusa's head to the king and queen and their guests; and ended when they obliged him by falling silent and dying, one by one by one.

Andromeda wept bitterly, her sobs unnaturally loud in the hall's stony hush. I suppose she was grieving for her parents, though they had treated her very badly. Mortals are odd that way.

"What happened?" A man's voice came from a corner, startling us all. "Tell me!" It was Molpus the singer, who had been saved by his blindness. His appearance so astonished Andromeda that she stopped crying.

"Tell me everything!" he demanded, turning his head this way and that like an inquisitive bird.

"Everything? That would take a long time."

"Tell me so I can sing of it," insisted Molpus.

"Will you remember?" Perseus asked, almost sternly.

"I am a poet," Molpus replied, with just a hint of sharpness.

So Perseus began his story, telling of Polydectes' passion for Danae, of Danae's resistance, and of Polydectes' request that Perseus bring him Medusa's head.

"Nobody has ever lived after seeing the Gorgon's face," said Molpus. "He was trying to kill you."

"Yes."

"But you survived," said Molpus. "How?"

Anticipating a glowing description of my incredible generosity, I wondered if I should stop Perseus before he wept with gratitude, thus saving him from embarrassing himself before his new bride. Zeus says I am capricious, but I am actually very thoughtful.

"The goddess Athena gave me her shield to use as a

mirror," said Perseus. "Without it I would have failed."

"Praise her!" cried Molpus piously. "Praise Athena the Wise, Athena the Warrior, Athena the Victor!"

"Praise her!" sang the newlyweds.

Praise her? I thought. *What about* me?

I began to make lists in my head.

What I Used to Think of Perseus

Clever

Clearheaded

Persistent

Nimble

Daring

What I Think of Him Now

Stupid

Ungrateful

Addled

Disloyal

Smelly

I toyed with the idea of turning him into a skunk, just to teach him a lesson. But before I could do anything, he said, "As grateful as I am to Athena, I owe even more to Hermes, my half brother," so I forbore.

"Your half brother?" Andromeda stared at her new husband as if he had just turned to gold. Few things are more entrancing to mortal women than the possibility that their men are Zeus' offspring. The faintest whiff of divinity makes them swoon.

"Yes." Then—finally!—Perseus returned to the vital subject of what I had done and how wonderful I was. Listening, Molpus nodded and swayed, as if hearing music. Once or twice he interjected, "Praise Hermes! Praise the Song Maker!" This pleased me greatly. Not all poets remember that I invented the lyre and the pipes, though they should, considering how dreary their lives would be without them.

Perseus went on, lauding me with agreeable frequency. By the time he finished describing the death of Medusa, the appearance of Pegasus, and our cloud-swept journey from Arcadia to Joppa, he and his audience were positively a-tremble with devotion.

It seemed like the perfect moment to reveal myself, so I did.

SEVENTEEN

Andromeda moaned as if she were about to faint, then sank to her knees, dropping forward so that her forehead knocked the floor. Perseus exclaimed with such genuine pleasure that my annoyance with him melted away like spring frost. And Molpus fairly shook with awe once he learned who I was. It was all very agreeable.

After a round of worshipful introductions, I commended Perseus for his actions.

"You have been heroic," I said, just to see if he would blush. He did. So did Andromeda, very prettily. Molpus was listening hard to every word, memorizing for future audiences, so I added that Perseus had another, equally daunting task ahead of him. "He must confront Polydectes," I said.

Andromeda blinked rapidly. The threat of losing her brand-new, semi-divine husband, after all she had experienced that day, was clearly testing her limits.

"He will face the task bravely and perform it well," I assured her. "Won't you?" I asked Perseus.

"I will," he vowed, looking at his bride. Her eyes were brimming.

"Polydectes will never dream you have the head," I said, for her benefit as much as his. "You'll surprise him, and the whole thing will be over before you can say 'large-animal sacrifice.' Meanwhile, I'll take Andromeda to your mother. She'll be safe there."

Leaving the newlyweds to say their farewells, I guided Molpus out of the palace. His sandals were worn, his robes threadbare, and he himself was very thin. Judging by his appearance, the life of a poet was not an easy one.

When we reached the doorway, I touched his forehead, giving him the gift of perfect memory.

"To help you sing of this," I said, opening the door.

After I picked up the sickle and reclaimed Pegasus, our journey to Seriphos went swiftly. Andromeda and I rode Pegasus, and Perseus followed wearing my sandals. The princess was silent all the way from Joppa to Crete—out of exhaustion or shyness, I could not tell. When we flew over the Sea of Cyrene, I urged her to rest and then composed a little tune for Pegasus. It was about mares romping in fields of sweet grass, their arching necks and flying tails. I crooned it to him, and his ears flicked back and forth in enjoyment, which was very satisfying. I like a good audience.

When I saw the broad shape of Lower Hellas below us, I said to Andromeda, "We're not far from

Seriphos. There it is, to the east." I pointed. "The small island shaped like a teardrop."

"I see it," she said quietly. Then she asked, "Is Perseus Danae's only son?"

"Only child," I said. "Much beloved."

"Ah." I heard worry in her voice. No doubt she was wondering how Danae would receive her and expecting the worst.

She's a far better woman than your mother was, I thought, but I said, "You two have a lot in common. Danae will welcome you as her daughter."

This was true. I saw a brief image, framed by shimmering patches of light, of Danae embracing Andromeda tearfully. This was the way my prophetic gift worked, in bright mind pictures that came and went as unexpectedly as sneezes. I had never been able to summon the Sight, the way Apollo could; mine had a will of its own. Seeing the future this way was more like an irritating physical ailment than a power. Still, I had learned to trust what I saw: it always happened.

EIGHTEEN

As I predicted, Danae welcomed her new daughter-in-law with much tearful emotion, just as she had in my vision. Then the two women began conversing as if they had known each other all their lives. I tend to forget that all mortal women do this. Whenever I witness it, I am bemused.

"Excuse me," I said, cutting short a rapt discussion of Perseus' eating habits, "I must go." This was true. Ares would certainly be wanting his sickle by now. "When he returns from the palace, tell Perseus to leave my sandals—"

"The palace! Is that where he is?" exclaimed Danae with horror.

"Of course," I replied. "He's giving Poly—" I got no

further: Danae, clutching Andromeda's arm, fell to her knees, pulling the poor girl down with her.

"Lord Hermes!" she cried. "Help my son! Polydectes is a brute! He's capable of anything. He may kill Perseus on sight!"

"But he has Medusa's—"

"Help him, I beg you!" Andromeda heard Danae's pleas and stiffened. Then she, who had endured so much that day with unshakable composure, suddenly lost every shred of it and began to shriek. Her awful cries inspired Danae to scream even louder.

I should have dropped the girl in a tree and kept on going, I thought, clapping my hands over my ears. I can't bear dissonance.

"All right, all right," I told them, "I'll make sure he's safe! Just stop your wailing!" I left before they could think of anything else to cry about and jumped onto Pegasus. As we flew to the palace, I told myself that their fears were groundless, that Perseus, by now an old hand at wielding Medusa's head, had overcome Polydectes with ease. But I hurried inside anyway and found the throne room as quickly as I could.

It was utterly silent. Perseus stood before Polydectes with eyes averted, showing him Medusa's head. Her glare had done its work, preserving every detail of the king's astonished rage, down to the dangerously swollen veins on his forehead. If she had killed him before apoplexy could, it mattered little now. He was well and truly dead.

Those few guards who had dutifully come forward to help their master were stone now, too, as were the others in the room: a servant girl bringing wine, a little boy with a finger up his nose, and a man with the weathered face and bandy legs of a groom. Only Perseus was still alive. Seeing me, he murmured a greeting.

"Well done, Perseus!" I said. "Your kin will rejoice.

They await you anxiously." *To say the very least,* I thought.

"I am glad that this is over." His voice was somber, deeper than before.

"Well, then, hurry home! But first give me my sandals." He removed them quickly. "And the head," I added, for he still held it. Eyes downcast, he coaxed the snakes off his wrist and worked the head into the leather pouch. When it was covered safely, he raised it to his heart, as a priest does with sacred libations. His face worked with guilt and sorrow. It was a painful combination, as I knew.

"I—Medusa saved my life three times," he faltered. "After I—I . . ." He couldn't say it: *After I cut off her head.*

"You had to do it." I made my voice brisk. "You had no choice. Anyway, you're a hero now. Things could be worse."

At this his mouth twitched halfheartedly. It was a

feeble effort at a smile, but an effort nonetheless. "Promise me you won't forget to offer to Athena," I said, tying on my sandals. "You've seen what happens when she takes offense."

"I promise."

"Good." I touched his shoulder the way Zeus so often touched mine, giving him my warmest blessing. Then I flew back to Olympus to return Ares' sickle.

From that day on, I never killed again.

PART THREE

Mount Ida

NINETEEN

I returned home with a light heart. Zeus would praise me for my brilliant work with Perseus. Throngs of beautiful, elusive, horse-loving dryads would vie for introductions to Pegasus. After showing him off to my heart's content, I would take a long, well-deserved rest.

How wrong I was.

Zeus, slumped on his wide marble throne, greeted me morosely. I wondered if I should try to cheer him with a joke, maybe the one about the mortal crossing the road. Before I could even open my mouth, he launched into a dark monologue about his least favorite child. Of many hundreds, her name was at the bottom of the list.

"Eris," he said, fairly spitting her name, "has really

gone too far this time. I'd hurl her down to Tartarus, but Hades would never forgive me."

Eris, Ares' pretty little sister, liked to stir up trouble. It was said that she'd persuaded Pandora to open the Box of All Woes, loosing misery on the world, and that she tattled to Hera whenever Zeus was unfaithful, loosing considerable misery on him.

"What did she do?"

"Came to Peleus' wedding uninvited, brought a golden apple inscribed 'To the Fairest,' and pitched it right at the feet of Hera, Athena, and Aphrodite."

Ouch! I thought. The goddesses, all famously vain, were always competing with each other. "Let me guess. Each of them claimed it."

"Exactly."

"What a troublemaker she is!" I said, awed by her terrible cleverness. Whatever Eris' reason for setting the goddesses against each other, she'd devised the perfect way of doing it. No wonder her nickname was Discord.

"It's her only gift," said Zeus with distaste, adding that Hera, Athena, and Aphrodite were no longer speaking. After disagreeing, bickering, and then quarreling over the apple, they'd resorted to high-decibel insults. Each of them had produced at least one memorable slur before stalking off in a fury. (Athena to Aphrodite: "You have the brain of a bedbug." Aphrodite to Athena: "Go shave your mustache.")

Now Olympus rang with an ominous silence.

"Where's the apple?" I asked. Zeus drew it from his robe. It was a pretty thing to have caused so much unpleasantness. Then again, the same could be said of Eris. "Hera won't give me a moment's peace," Zeus complained. "She's pushing me to make the decision."

"And give her the apple?"

His lip curled in assent. "I can't do it, of course. I told her I'd arrange a contest."

"A beauty contest? Good idea."

"A fair beauty contest."

"Even better."

"So we have to find a fair judge."

We? Olympian rivalries make me queasy—they're unpleasant and dangerous, even to innocent bystanders. "I'm sure you'll think of the perfect person," I said, eyeing the doorway.

But Zeus clapped me on the shoulder and shook me. "Think!" he urged. "You're clever! Who would be truly impartial?"

I was stuck. "Well," I mused, "if it's impartial we want, scratch the Immortals. As for generals and warriors, scratch them, too—they'd choose Athena." The Goddess of Wisdom, a great military strategist, was adored by fighting men. They called her Athena, Hope of Soldiers.

"You're right. She'd promise them invincibility." Zeus knew his daughter well.

Because Hera granted riches and power to those she favored, I said, "No rulers or politicians, either—they'd pick your wife."

"Right again."

"So that leaves us with the humbler folk," I said. "Farmers, shepherds, poets—"

"Shepherds?" Zeus snapped his fingers. "Wait! I've got it! There's a shepherd in Troy who'd be perfect."

"Really? Who?"

"Paris," said Zeus. "Second son of Troy's royal family, though he doesn't know it. Thinks he's a mountain boy. One of those raised-in-obscurity-for-their-own-good mortals, like Atalanta, Jason, Perseus . . ."

As Zeus spoke, the Sight came to me. A handsome, dark-haired young man stood on a pile of rubble. Devastation raged around him. Towers flamed, bodies fell through red smoke. The rubble, I saw, was layered with corpses.

The image disappeared as suddenly as it had come, leaving me with an aching gut and a dry mouth. It was a moment before I could speak. Then I said, "He's handsome?"

"As a god! Even the sheep are lovesick!" declared Zeus, slapping his thigh cheerfully. "He's the most beautiful of mortals. So of course he should choose the most beautiful goddess! Excellent! I'm glad I thought of him."

I will always regret what happened next. The Sight had shown me Paris against a backdrop of disaster. I should have guessed that his judging had brought him there, and brought on the disaster, too.

I wasn't quick enough. My nimble wits failed me, and the chance to suggest another judge was lost. Much else was lost, too, as I would come to learn. But at that moment, when Zeus said imperiously, "Don't just stand there, Hermes! Get moving! Bring Paris the good news!" I felt I had no choice, and I obeyed.

TWENTY

He was indeed beautiful, a slim, peachy-skinned youth with dark eyes and long lashes. Such folk cause hearts to flutter and minds to stall. They command adoring attention, even if they're doing something trivial, and so it was with Paris. When I arrived on Mount Ida, after a long, sky-coursing run in my winged sandals, he was lying in a meadow, surrounded by his flock. A lovely young nymph—a river girl, to judge by her webbed hands and feet—crouched behind him, assiduously picking lice out of his hair. The sheep, the nymph, and the lice, too, for all I knew, were alert to his every move.

When he shifted, the nymph implored him to be still, rapping him gently with her fine-toothed wooden comb. "Paris, please! I'm almost finished." He shrugged restlessly. "Are you too warm?" she asked with concern. He nodded, pouting. "As soon as I'm done, I'll fan you," she promised, and he sighed. Then, like a child trading good behavior for a sweet, he closed his eyes and lay perfectly still. He was even more beautiful in repose.

At length the nymph put down her comb. "There. All done. The lice love you almost as much as I do." She kissed the top of his head.

Paris smiled, sat up, and scratched his head vigorously. The nymph handed him a vial of sweet oil, and he ran the stuff through his hair. Then he took to twisting his fine dark curls into long ringlets, tossing them over his shoulder one by one until they covered his back like an exotic pelt. He did this with total self-absorption, and the nymph watched, enthralled.

She loves him and he loves him, I thought. *But will it last?* Long years of escorting the dead down to Hades had taught me that such pairings often end in murderous rage, at least on one side. At present, though, these two seemed quite content.

I whipped off my Cap of Invisibility to make them jump, and they did. It's a cheap trick, but sometimes I can't resist.

"Lord Hermes!" Paris knelt with easy grace.

"Good day," I said. "You are Paris?"

"I am."

"And you are—?" I asked the nymph.

"Oenone," she said, "of the river Oenus."

I recognized the name; I had heard it from Apollo. Long ago, when he himself was living as a shepherd, he'd taken a liking to the nymph and taught her the art of healing. *And now you devote your time to Paris*, I thought, *who doesn't seem to appreciate you*.

"I come with a message from All-Powerful Zeus," I told Paris, and his eyes widened. "He wants you to judge a contest."

"Livestock?" he asked eagerly.

"Not exactly," I replied. "Beauty."

I told him about the apple and its inscription and the uproar it had caused on Olympus. "Because you possess great beauty yourself, Zeus thinks you can be impartial in the judging of it," I said.

A rosy flush crept up his neck. "I—I am so surprised!" he said with emotion. "This is a great honor! And—and I will do my best to be fair and impartial, as Lord Zeus wishes." He touched his hand to his heart, as men do when they make a vow.

Until this moment Oenone's eyes had never left Paris; now they closed, hard. *She's afraid of losing him,* I thought. *And she may.* The nymph was lovely, but the goddesses were magnificent, and all of them had dallied with mortals—even, it was rumored, solemn, virginal Athena. Seducing mortals was one of the great guilty pleasures of the gods, second only to tipping cattle and ruining the weather. Paris might tempt any one of them. He did not seem the type to resist any beautiful female, much less a divine one.

I pitied Oenone.

"The goddesses may try to sway you," I warned Paris, knowing it was more than a possibility. "Don't let them!"

"I won't, I swear," he promised.

TWENTY-ONE

I can't really blame Paris for what happened next. He did try to be fair. But the goddesses were at their worst that day—working the poor fellow like wet clay, twisting and bending and pulling at him until he didn't know what to think. It was sad. And I couldn't do anything about it, because I wasn't supposed to be there.

I meant to return to Olympus after escorting the goddesses to Mount Ida, truly I did; once they had met Paris, my job was over. But after introducing everyone, saying goodbye, and bounding into the air, I changed my mind. The three Immortal Ones, fixed on Paris like cobras on a baby bird, looked so resolute, so splendid!

Why shouldn't I watch? I thought. *There's no harm in*

it. I was flying over a stand of tall cypresses, hidden from view, when I decided. So I put on my Cap of Invisibility, doubled back to the spot where Paris stood with the divine trio, and settled down to spectate.

I had barely made myself comfortable when Aphrodite did what she does best: she disrobed.

"You can judge me better this way," she said to Paris, shrugging off her diaphanous gown and stepping out of her tiny golden sandals. "Don't you think?" She turned with practiced languor, showing off her glorious body, which was bare except for her magic girdle. Fashioned by Hephaestus of fine gold mesh set with gems, the girdle made its wearer completely irresistible. Hera borrowed it sometimes when she wanted Zeus' undivided attention, but it usually stayed where it belonged, around Aphrodite's waist. At the moment, it was having a very strong effect on Paris. He looked as if he'd been poleaxed.

Hera and Athena looked stunned also, but for a different reason. They never gave Aphrodite much credit for intelligence—they considered her an ornamental scatterbrain—and now she'd truly put them on the spot. Unclothed, she was as radiant as an ocean pearl, and Paris' eyes were riveted to her. His shapely legs actually wobbled. If Hera and Athena didn't undress too, he'd never even look at them.

Hera made up her mind first.

"What a clever idea," she purred, throwing a very polished, very insincere smile in Aphrodite's direction. "I should have thought of it myself. Though you really must take off your girdle, Aphrodite. It's giving you an unfair advantage."

"I agree," said Athena, who had gone as far as removing her gauntlets.

"Ooh, we can't have that." Aphrodite's husky sarcasm was not lost on her rivals, who waited pointedly for her to pull off the girdle. This she did slowly, almost teasingly. The girdle slithered to the ground, and Athena glared at it.

Now Hera moved closer to Paris, undoing the brooches and pins that fastened her robes. As she approached him, they drifted onto the grass like great silken petals, until she was entirely bare. I'd never seen her like this, and I was impressed: she was stately and voluptuous, her incandescent skin a testament to milk baths, royal jelly, and massage.

Even so, Paris seemed more inclined to look at Aphrodite. In her girdle or out of it, she was bewitching. I myself never failed to pulse with longing when she smiled at me, even though she'd been doing it for centuries. She was having the same effect on Paris.

Undaunted, Hera took his arm.

"Come. Let's chat," she said, leading him to a spot very near me. On the way she managed to retrieve her shawl, and now she draped the purple silk around herself in such a way—slowly, carefully—that Paris' eyes were drawn to her bosom. She gave him a few moments to appreciate its gentle rise and fall, its bounteous contours, its perfume. When he was fully attentive, she said, "I'm impressed with you, Paris, really I am. I know a born leader when I see one."

"You do?"

"Oh, yes. Believe me, you're not what you think you are. You're destined for great things. Fate has much more in store for you than this. . . ." She gestured dismissively toward the flock.

"Really?" Something in his voice told me he might have entertained such thoughts himself. Shepherds often daydream—about riches, about glory, about life without biting insects. According to Apollo, they all think they're destined to lead men, not sheep. He calls it an occupational delusion, whatever that is.

". . . provided you make the right decisions," Hera continued, "if you catch my drift."

Paris swallowed. "Uh . . . what are you . . . I mean, are you saying that . . . ?" Behind that perfect forehead, the mind was struggling.

"I'm saying that I can give you power and riches if you give me the apple," Hera replied smoothly. "Think about it." She gave him the full benefit of her turquoise gaze. "You'll be a prince of Troy and live in a palace of at least two stories, perhaps even three. You'll have hot food. Warm baths. Fine clothing. Personal groomers. People will obey you. They'll satisfy your every whim." She leaned toward him, leading with her breasts. "There's absolutely nothing like it," she whispered. "Nothing!"

"It sounds wonderful," Paris said enthusiastically. "Warm baths? Fine clothes? I would give almost anything . . ." He caught himself. "But . . . I swore to Hermes and Lord Zeus that I'd judge fairly. So I really can't accept . . ." He faltered, swiping at the droplets of sweat on his brow. Not quite daring to look Hera in the eye, he asked, "Did . . . did you say personal groomers?"

"As many as you like," she assured him.

His handsome face puckered with indecision. "Well—"

"Excuse me for interrupting." Athena, bareheaded and wearing only her white linen undergarments, appeared between them suddenly.

"Oh! You frightened me!" cried Hera.

"Really." The Goddess of Wisdom, self-possessed even in her underwear, did not apologize. "Your husband has arrived," she said crisply. "He's come as an eagle, and he's waiting for you." She pointed. A fierce-looking bird surveyed the countryside from the top of the tallest cypress. Zeus often took the form of an eagle. He liked the improved eyesight—it helped him to find pretty girls. But sometimes he just felt like soaring. Perhaps today was one of those days.

"Then I must go." Unless Zeus had been philandering—at which times she let loose like an undammed river—Hera was a model wife. She retreated hastily but not before mouthing the words "Personal groomers!" to Paris behind Athena's back.

TWENTY-TWO

The Goddess of Wisdom waited until Hera was out of earshot. Then she said to Paris, "I've come under false pretenses. I lied. That bird's not really Zeus. But I know as surely as I sprang full-grown from Zeus' head that Hera's been trying to bribe you." She waited for Paris to deny this. When he didn't, she said, "As I suspected. I was right to stop her. If she's inventing new rules for this contest, we all get to play by them. Including me."

Right you are, I thought. Athena has her faults, but she is nobody's fool.

"Now," she said, straightening and raising her chin commandingly, "judge my beauty."

"Y-yes, Goddess." Paris stepped back, and so did she. After standing for a moment with her knees locked and her hands at her sides, she turned stiffly in place. When she was once again facing Paris, she halted. Staring straight ahead like a soldier on review, she allowed him to inspect her. "Here I am," she seemed to be saying, "so pay attention."

Athena's erect bearing and no-nonsense delivery were about as seductive as an ice bath, and her voice was field commander–brusque. But her brow was noble, and her hair, which was always tucked into her helmet, proved to be thick and heavy, a pure silvery white that was startling against her smooth, sun-browned skin. Her wide-set gray eyes—Zeus called them "all-seeing"—shone like silver. Free of armor, her long, straight limbs were lithe and strong, lovely to see. It had never occurred to me that Athena was beautiful. Now I saw that she was. *All this and a mind like a bronze trap*, I thought. *Well, well.*

"Have you finished?" she asked Paris crisply.

"Yes, Goddess."

"Then I'll be brief. You look like a sensible fellow. You must want advancement in the world; it's only natural."

He nodded, simply to agree with her, I think. Her manner said it was foolish not to.

"Good. I can promise you a generalship, forty horses, and an unbroken string of military victories. Entire territories will fall to you. Shrines will be raised in your honor. I'll have my very own armorer make you a sword. He's a genius. You'll be free to plunder and maraud at will. And you can storm out of meetings whenever you like—all in exchange for the apple. What do you say?"

Once again Paris' brow was beaded with sweat. He wiped it away and collected himself before replying. "I—I thank you for your offer," he said slowly. "It's most generous. But"—and here he took a very deep breath—"I'm not a military man, Goddess. The truth is, I don't really like to fight. I've never even wanted a sword."

Athena stared at him as if he'd just coughed up a lizard. But before she could say anything, Hera descended.

"You lied to me, Athena!" she hissed. "That wasn't Zeus, it was a field hawk, and you knew it!" She turned on Paris. "What's she been saying to you?" she demanded.

Athena gave a nearly imperceptible shake of her head, warning Paris to keep silent. If Hera learned that he'd rejected her offer, she'd gloat, and Athena couldn't tolerate that. Seeing Athena's warning look, Paris had the good sense to hold his tongue, but Hera pressed him. "Well?" she asked sharply.

At this moment a melodious "Eu-hoo!" came from Aphrodite, who was once again clothed, sandaled, girdled, and waiting under the cypresses. "What are you doing over there?" she called. "Is the contest over?"

"Not yet," responded Paris. Seizing the chance to escape before Hera questioned him further, he bolted and was at Aphrodite's side before anyone could stop him. The Love Goddess greeted him warmly and asked him something that none of us could hear. He responded with a shake of his head, which seemed to please her.

Meanwhile, Hera and Athena stood near me, seething. The air between them fairly rippled with bad feeling, and I wondered if they'd start arguing again. I half hoped they would—I was still sorry I'd missed their slang fest over the apple.

But at that moment we all saw Aphrodite pull Paris down beside her and whisper in his ear. Whatever she said made him nod happily, which he continued to do even as Athena and Hera, noting this exchange and fearing the worst, bore down on him together.

They were too late.

By the time they reached Paris, he had made his judgment, and the coveted golden apple lay in Aphrodite's lap.

TWENTY-THREE

Everyone behaved well, at first.

"I see you've won, Aphrodite," said Athena as Paris helped the victor to her rosy little feet. "Congratulations."

"Thank you, Athena. I *am* pleased," replied Aphrodite, emphasizing her victory by fondling the apple ever so gently. "Though I know Paris had a very hard time making his decision." Her sea-green eyes gleamed under her lashes as she delivered this patently false statement, which ended with the hint of a mischievous smile.

"Is that so." It was not really a question. "Tell us how you made it," Hera said to Paris. "That is, if you don't mind."

"Yes, do," seconded Athena, planting herself next to

Hera so that their arms touched. Surprisingly, neither backed away. There was a new alliance forming between the two sore-losing goddesses, a formidable one. *Doesn't bode well*, I thought, not knowing exactly why.

"Well, uh, you are all very beautiful," Paris began, "and I would give an apple to each of you if I could, believe me." He offered them a quick, ingratiating smile, but Hera and Athena remained unaffected.

This must be a first for handsome Paris, I thought. He'd probably never met resistance in his life—never from a female, at any rate.

He swallowed nervously, squirming under the searing stares of the two goddesses. "But as that isn't possible," he continued, "I, uh . . ." He gave up, casting a pleading glance at Aphrodite instead. Whatever her promises to him, they had not covered this—two powerful, resentful goddesses, simmering hotly in defeat.

He looked as if he wanted to jump into a hole.

Then Aphrodite—in her leisurely fashion—came to his rescue.

"Oh, all right," she said, heaving an exasperated sigh, "I'll tell you if you really want to know. I think Paris deserves the most beautiful woman in the world. After all, he's the handsomest man. It seems only fitting."

Paris' rapturous expression said that he agreed completely.

"And they'd make such a dazzling couple," Aphrodite went on. "Like gods! Or demigods at the very least. . . . So that's what I promised—the love of the world's most beautiful woman."

"*That's* what you chose?" Athena asked, with mingled scorn and disbelief.

"Helen of Sparta?" asked Hera, at the very same moment.

Aphrodite stared at Hera. "How did *you* know?" she demanded.

"I know more than you think," replied Hera with an air of mystery.

You know because you watch your husband like a hawk, I thought. My guess was that Zeus had mentioned Helen's beauty at one time or another, and jealous Hera had never forgotten it. Unlike Athena, Hera had a prodigious memory, especially when it came to her husband's roving eye. She could reel off the names of all the girls he'd chased for the last three hundred years. She'd tormented many of them personally.

"Has Aphrodite mentioned that Helen is married?" Hera asked Paris. "No—let me guess—she forgot to tell you."

Paris' flawless jaw dropped, confirming Hera's suspicions. "Shame on you, Aphrodite!" She wagged her finger playfully, but there was venom in her voice. "You've deceived the judge!"

"You really are despicable," commented Athena,

who was once again wearing her breastplate and helmet.

"Oh, stop it!" protested Aphrodite. "The two of you are such hypocrites! What claim do you have to the moral high ground? None! You tried to bribe him, too, I'd stake my girdle on it. You're just angry because he took my offer instead of yours."

Neither goddess responded. "You see," she said to Paris, "they don't deny it." She gave him a reassuring pat on the back. "Yes, it's true, Helen is married, but Menelaus is a terrible husband. Most of the time he ignores her. If not, he's showing her off to his kinsmen like a trophy. The woman is lonely. She needs some loving attention. And when you offer it, Paris, believe me, she'll follow you anywhere—even to Troy."

I couldn't believe that Aphrodite would really fulfill her promise, but Paris was practically panting with eagerness. *You're in for a big disappointment*, I thought.

Good thing you have Oenone, though you don't deserve her.

"If you think it's going to be that easy, you're even stupider than I thought," Athena muttered, crouching to buckle up her greaves.

"What did you say?" snapped Aphrodite.

Athena's reply was a quick, contemptuous shake of her head. She turned to Hera and they shared a look of dark complicity. Then, all differences forgotten, they linked arms, nodded a curt farewell to Paris, and—without saying a word to Aphrodite—strode away together.

There's a not-so-pretty picture, I thought, watching them go. The alliance of Hera and Athena against Aphrodite disturbed me, and I found myself wondering what they would do to punish her.

But Aphrodite paid them no mind. She was used to getting her way, and if her caprices caused trouble, she refused to worry—there were more amusing things to do. Besides, worrying caused unsightly frown lines. I had heard her say so myself.

Now, happy with her stolen victory and oblivious to its consequences, she coaxed Paris into a game of catch-and-toss with her shiny new toy.

TWENTY-FOUR

I reported to Zeus right away.

"Aphrodite, eh?" He lowered his voice, though we were alone in the throne room. "Hera would kill me for saying this," he confided, "but Aphrodite really is the fairest." I told him how she'd disrobed, forcing Hera and Athena to follow suit, and he smiled broadly.

"Athena undressed? Good thing you were wearing your cap, son. She might have run you through!" Then he caught himself. "Or are you teasing me?"

As we strolled out of the throne room, I assured him I was telling the truth, and after many extravagant oaths—I even swore on my sandals—he believed me. By then we were on the western parapet, a large circular overhang paved with malachite. My father liked to sit here at sunset with a goblet of ambrosia; every now and then he invited me to join him. It always felt like a privilege, a reward for some accomplishment or other, though he seldom praised me. When he did, I cherished his words. When he didn't, I enjoyed sitting with him in amicable silence, admiring the view. From these heights earth and its deep blue oceans looked both picturesque and deceptively serene.

Now Zeus took his favorite lapis chair, patting the one beside it. I sat. "I'm pleased this thing has been resolved," he said. "It's definitely cleared the air. I could hardly believe my eyes when I saw Hera and Athena walking arm in arm a few hours ago, whispering like schoolgirls." He shook his head. "I can't imagine what they were talking about, but at least they weren't squabbling."

They were plotting against Aphrodite, I thought, wanting very badly to tell him about my misgivings, yet reluctant to cloud this happy moment. Then he smiled and said, "You did well, son," and in my infinite pleasure at his words the thought flew out of my head.

The next day my misgivings about the goddesses returned, and when I couldn't find Aphrodite, I decided to visit Apollo. My brother isn't only the God of Prophecy, he also has the ability to view things clearly, no matter what he feels about them. I was not above mocking his cool, dispassionate ways, but when I needed a good, sharp insight or two, I always sought him out. His mind is as keen as a blade.

I found him in one of his many hunting camps on the forested slopes of Olympus. Apollo likes to rough it. He will sometimes retreat to the wilderness for weeks on end, eating mushrooms, drinking only water, no wine, and sleeping on the ground with his dogs.

They barked madly when I appeared out of the air.

"Greetings, Lord of the Silver Bow," I said, landing on a tree trunk and bowing deeply.

"Wayfinder! You found me!" he retorted, and we both smiled. I told him he was looking very fit—he was—and asked him if he happened to know where Aphrodite was.

His smile faded. "Gone to Sparta," he said. "Took Eros with her."

"Really?"

"Mischief is brewing."

I heaved a sigh. My brother and I are very different. He is sober; I am cheerful. He sees darkness coming when my skies are bright. His gift of prophecy is strong and reliable; mine is fitful. We often disagree. But at this moment we saw eye to eye. Eros, Aphrodite's son, would shoot Helen with one of his golden arrows, making her fall head over heels in love with Paris. With this, Aphrodite's promise to Paris would be fulfilled.

The adoring couple would be happy.

The rest of the world would not.

When I told him everything that had happened on Mount Ida, Apollo said, "If Helen runs off with Paris, Menelaus won't stand for it. Neither will his brother, Agamemnon. They'll call on all their Achaean allies and go after her."

Paris' homeland was a long way from Sparta—on the eastern side of the Aegean. "To Troy?"

He nodded. "They're fighting men, they've been itching for a brawl, and Troy is famed for its riches. Helen's desertion would be the perfect excuse to attack."

I knew, even before he said the word, what that meant: war.

PART FOUR

The Trojan Plain

TWENTY-FIVE

Apollo's prediction came true. Handsome Paris fell in love with beautiful Helen and enticed her to Troy. Helen's husband, Menelaus, helped by his brother, Agamemnon, mustered an army and sailed across the Aegean to bring her back. When their great black warships were beached within sight of Troy's walls, Menelaus demanded his wife's return.

She refused, and the fighting began.

Naturally, the Immortals took sides.

Aphrodite, Apollo, and Artemis backed Paris and the Trojans; Athena, Hera, and Poseidon supported Menelaus and the Greeks.

Ares helped both armies; he was the God of War,

after all, and he reveled in organized carnage. So when he figured out that the war would last much longer if he helped everybody, that's what he did. First he fought with the Trojans. After a few years, he switched to the Greeks.

Once, grinning down at the fighting, he shouted, "I hope it goes on forever!" I liked him even less after that.

I wanted no part of the war and remained neutral, as did Demeter and Hades. I was hoping my father would stay out of it, too, but I hoped in vain—as soon as the fighting began, he allied himself with the Trojans. Perhaps it was out of loyalty to Paris, his choice to judge the goddesses, or to Paris' father, King Priam, his devoted worshiper. Whatever the reason, Zeus helped them win a string of battles, which enraged Hera and Athena and saddened me. In my opinion, his actions set a bad example for the other gods. If he'd remained aloof, they might have restrained themselves, too. But he didn't, so they didn't, either.

While they fanned the flames of war and danced around the fire, I skulked in the shadows, choking on my objections.

And then there was my guilt.

Gods don't suffer guilt, because they never question themselves. Self-examination is beneath them. After all, they're perfect.

I seemed to be the exception.

When the fighting began, a voice in my head kept whispering that I was far from perfect, that I could have prevented the war if only I'd kept Paris from judging the three goddesses. It was an insistent, coldly emphatic voice, and I didn't want to believe it, but I did. It made me feel terrible, worse than when I'd killed Argos so long ago, worse than when I'd watched Medusa die. It was as if I'd been assigned my own private Fury or found myself afflicted with some painful, shameful disease.

I fell into a state of perpetual gloom. The other gods

avoided me—I couldn't stop complaining about the war or trying to convince them to stay out of it. Hera told me I'd turned into a hideous bore. Ares was less gracious; he threatened to split my skull with an ax. Zeus heard me out exactly once. Then, for some reason, he never had time for me again.

So I drifted away, and nobody noticed.

I told myself I was needed elsewhere. And that's how I ended up back in Hell, working like a donkey.

Every soldier killed in battle—and there were throngs of them—had to be escorted to the Underworld. This was my responsibility as Head Psychopomp. So if I wasn't in Taenarus Cave greeting the dead, I was leading them down to the River Styx. It was back and forth, back and forth, every day, all day. I was at the riverbank so often that Cerberus stopped growling at me. He even wagged his tail once or twice.

That made me feel worse.

I reflected morosely that guiding the dead had once been easy, humdrum work—almost boring. Before the war, most of my charges were old and feeble, more than ready for a nice long rest in the Asphodel Fields. I joked with them, they laughed and smiled, and we all had a fine time.

No longer. Now the dead were men in their prime, or youths, or smooth-faced boys, who staggered into the cave coated with dirt and blood. Greeks and Trojans, they all came with mangled limbs, smashed skulls, and bright, gaping wounds, stupefied that their lives were over.

When they began to heal, on the way to the Underworld, they found their voices, too. Some told me urgently that they had fought hard and died bravely. Others wept for their families. Still others voiced regret or confusion or shame. I gave what consolation I could.

"You died with honor," I said; or, "Your kin will always remember you."

A few were bitter. They always asked the same question: "Why?" It always filled me with dread, because I'd never been able to come up with a soothing answer. So I'd tell them it was Fate and change the subject.

One day, when I found myself idle for a moment, I sat down and made a pair of lists.

Bad Things About War

Constant bickering and scheming on Olympus
Widespread suffering on earth
Hordes of unhappy dead needing escort service
Overcrowding in Asphodel Fields
No time to play music
No time to ride Pegasus

Good Things About War

Ares overjoyed

Eris elated

Hades happy

Dismal, I thought. And that was the end of my list making.

TWENTY-SIX

One day a small crowd of Trojan dead shambled into the cave. This surprised me. Lately the Trojans had been gaining the advantage, driving the Greeks back to their warships, even setting one afire. Hector, King Priam's favorite son, had led the attack against the ships. "We're driving those mongrel dogs away!" he exulted, and it seemed he was right.

But on this particular day, forty-seven Trojan soldiers appeared, bringing news that the tide had turned. Achilles, Greece's greatest warrior, had just killed Hector in single combat. This was a terrible blow to the Trojans: they loved Hector as only people under siege can love a strong protector.

And now, to their horror, Achilles had tied

Hector's body to his chariot and was dragging it around the city walls. The prince, he swore, would never have a proper burial; his corpse would go to the dogs and crows.

It was an act of defilement so obscenely vengeful that even the gods were taken aback.

"Steal it."

"What?"

"You're the Prince of Thieves; steal Hector's body. Achilles is destroying it." Apollo and I were outside Taenarus Cave. It was dawn, one of the few times of day I was idle, and my brother stood before me with stubble on his jaw and shadows under his eyes. He looked as if he'd been awake for days and was so lackluster that he could have passed for a mortal.

I stared at him in disbelief. "Who sent you?" I asked, wondering if it was Zeus, hoping it was.

"Artemis and Aphrodite and I talked it over. We decided together." When I was silent, partly out of disappointment, Apollo said, "I know you want to keep your distance from the war, and I respect that. But won't you help just this once?" His knowing blue eyes held mine. "It's gotten really ugly."

I see the dead every day, I thought.

"I've missed you."

And I've missed you, I thought, but I didn't say it. Apollo hadn't bothered to seek me out since the war began—until this moment, when he wanted a favor.

"What you're asking is impossible," I said curtly.

He saw that I was angry, and he probably knew why. When he colored a little, I was pleased that I'd shamed him.

"Hera and Athena will torment me until the end of time if I help you. Surely you know that."

His color deepened. One of Apollo's most endearing

qualities is the ease with which he blushes. It happens when he's rattled or even thinking of lying. I suspect that's why he sticks to the truth—he knows his face will betray him.

"I do," he admitted. "But we're desperate. And Father isn't helping."

"Why not?" I couldn't help it. I was curious.

"I don't know. I thought he was fond of Priam, didn't you?"

I shrugged. "I assumed so. He backed Troy, after all."

"Well, you'd think he'd take pity on the man," said Apollo. "Ever since Hector died, Priam's been sitting in the palace courtyard, rocking back and forth and wailing. He won't sleep or eat, and it won't be long before he dies of heartbreak, unless . . ."

". . . he gets Hector's body back. Which requires help from Zeus. Who's withholding it," I finished. *Why I hate war,* I thought.

"Can't you think of a way to reach him?" asked Apollo. "You know him so well."

"*Knew*," I corrected. "*Knew* him so well. We haven't spoken since the war started. He wouldn't listen to me then. Why would he listen to me now?" Then I asked, "What about you? Why don't you talk to him?"

"Hera won't let me. She doesn't care if the body rots."

Typical, I thought. Hera and Athena still bore a huge grudge against Paris for the beauty contest on Mount Ida. They despised all Trojans, dead or alive.

"There must be a way to get around her," I mused, "some way to enlist Father's help without letting her know." And then it came to me. "Why not send him a dream?" Apollo had the power to send prophetic dreams, very persuasive ones. Their messages, whether hopeful or dire, were hard to ignore. Even Almighty Zeus might heed one.

Apollo considered it, then clapped me on the shoulder. "Good idea, Hermes!"

Coming from him, this was high praise indeed, and I warmed to it. "Meanwhile," I said, "tell Aphrodite to dress Hector's body so it doesn't decompose. Put her unguents and lotions to some good use for a change." Aphrodite had a store of cosmetics that could fill Ares' armory, everything from oil of musk to bat saliva. Their youth-enhancing properties were fabled. Aphrodite doled them out to the other goddesses in exchange for favors. Even the ageless were vain.

Apollo shook his head. "She won't budge from Olympus. She's been afraid to go anywhere near the fighting since she got hit." The Greek captain Diomedes had actually wounded Aphrodite early in the war, when she appeared in battle with the Trojans. No mortal had ever attacked a god before; it had caused such a stir that even I'd heard about it. *Get ready for an unhappy death,*

Diomedes, I remembered thinking, *because it's coming for you*.

"But Hector's body isn't on the battlefield," I said, repeating something I'd heard from one of the dead. "It's in the Greek camp, outside Achilles' tent."

"Of course!" Apollo smacked his forehead. "She'll be perfectly safe if she cloaks herself in fog. I'll remind her." He smiled at me gratefully. Now that he had a course of action, his radiance reemerged, and he fairly shone with purpose. "Thank you, brother."

Keep in touch, I thought, wondering if he would.

TWENTY-SEVEN

The next morning Iris, the Rainbow Goddess, came to see me, announcing her arrival with a flash of light and a whispered greeting. I wondered why I was getting so many live visitors all of a sudden. It was a little unsettling.

"Iris," I said. "Welcome! You're looking very well." This was a lie. Iris' chiton was ragged and splattered with blood, and her winged sandals were filthy. In fact, I had never seen her looking so bedraggled. She worked as Zeus' messenger when I wasn't around, and she was usually immaculate, radiating waves of brilliant, hypnotic color every time she moved.

"Thanks, but let's not waste our time on pleasantries," she said hoarsely. "Zeus wants to see you."

"He does?" I asked, with embarrassing eagerness.

"He does. Between you and me, I hope he's calling you back to work, because I'm worn out. I've been heralding for him *and* Hera, and they're running me ragged! First Zeus sends me down to the Trojans. Then Hera sends me down to the Greeks. I'm flying to earth five or six times a day! My voice is ruined, and I'm so tired I can hardly cast a decent rainbow anymore."

I made a sympathetic noise.

"I need a good long rest in some desert country," she said, "as far from Troy as I can get." She looked at me. "Don't just stand there, Hermes, put on your winged sandals! You know he doesn't like to be kept waiting."

Hera and Athena were in the audience hall when I got there, flanking Zeus' empty throne. A moment later Ares showed up, begrimed and armored, followed by

Apollo, Artemis, and Aphrodite. I was surprised and crestfallen; I had expected to see Zeus alone.

Then he strode into the hall, his solemn bearing deepening the silence around him. He sat. When I stepped forward, he nodded in greeting but did not rise, much less embrace me, though we hadn't seen each other in years. He was as distant as if I were the envoy of some obscure Druidic cult, come to invite him to the opening of a new rock circle.

I stepped back, appalled and trying not to show it.

Then his scepter flashed like winter lightning, and he spoke. "Achilles' desecration of Hector's body has gone on long enough," he pronounced. "It must stop. He will release the body for burial without delay. Hermes Wayfinder will oversee it."

This was Zeus in all his icy majesty, his voice ringing like a great bronze bell. I heard the anger in it—we all did—and wondered why he had chosen to summon me this way, before so many of the other gods. Then, seeing the frozen faces of Hera and Athena, I understood. Zeus was sending me on an errand, true, but he was also delivering a message to Achilles' most powerful supporters. By denouncing the Greek champion, he was telling Hera and Athena to stop interfering in the war.

I felt a long, sweet tingle of hope. I had never known Zeus to rebuke the goddesses this way. Could he be tiring of the war? Had he decided to end it somehow? "Let it be so," I murmured, and he looked at me. I thought I saw affection in his dark eyes, but I couldn't be sure.

"King Priam will go to Achilles tonight, with ransom for Hector's body," he decreed. "You, Hermes, will guide him there, keeping him safe behind enemy lines. When his business is finished, you will escort him back to Troy." The scepter flashed, dismissing me.

I bowed deeply. *That must have been some dream Apollo sent!* I thought, flying out of the hall.

TWENTY-EIGHT

In his day Priam had been a force to reckon with. He'd fathered fifty sons, an impressive number for a mortal. He'd been a sensible, pious king, offering generously to Zeus. And he'd amassed great riches, a fortune in gold and jewels that was said to be tucked away somewhere in the palace, nobody knew where. Priam kept its location secret from everyone, even his own family. The treasure was legendary, and the Greeks speculated endlessly about it.

And now the treasure is leaving, I thought.

It was nightfall. I hovered invisibly outside the city gates, watching Priam and his lone attendant Idaeus. Hours before, Zeus had sent the old king a message through Iris: Achilles would surrender Hector's body in exchange for a sizable ransom. "Give him enough to melt his rage" were Zeus' instructions, and Priam had obeyed.

Now Idaeus, an aging, blunt-faced fellow with hair as white as the king's, drove a donkey wagon heaped high with riches: woolen robes and blankets; bronze tripods; stacks of gold bars; amber, coral, and lapis beads; copper cauldrons; leopard skins; silver goblets. Truly a king's ransom, it was loaded atop the long wicker box that would serve as Hector's coffin.

If Priam had ever hoarded his riches, I reflected, *that time was over.*

The great city gates closed behind them. The king's stallions, hitched to his war chariot, pranced onto the plain with eye-rolling, pent-up energy. They'd been inside the walled city too long and wanted to run. Priam kept them reined in—he was a born horseman—but only with great effort.

Idaeus watched with concern, but he knew better than to suggest changing places with the king. Slaves drove donkeys; royalty did not. So Idaeus whipped his team until they took the lead. Priam's horses, forced to follow their lowly cousins, finally settled.

As they drove on, Idaeus peered ahead into the darkness, watching for Greek scouts or guards. Priam, on the other hand, seemed to be looking inward. Once or twice I saw his mournful eyes sweep the plain. I wondered if he was remembering Troy's glory days, when it was strong and prosperous. Perhaps he was picturing Hector out here, training his beloved horses.

Poor man, I thought.

After a time the moon rose, revealing the Greek encampment in the distance. A vast sprawl of men, animals, and rough-hewn dwellings, it extended all the way down to the beach. There were hundreds of tents; livestock pens and horse lines by the dozen; clusters of war chariots, some upturned for repair; cooking hearths; store sheds; and altars. Soldiers beyond counting lay on the ground asleep.

But *were* they asleep?

Priam and Idaeus, seeing what lay ahead of them, had come to a halt. Now the wind gusted their way, bringing a chorus of sighs, whispers, and drowsy chatter. But there were no snores. They exchanged a worried look. Many Greeks, it seemed, were still awake. It was easy to guess what the two men were thinking.

Zeus had promised them help in traveling safely to Achilles. Had he led them here only to betray them? Devout as Priam was, he knew all too well how fickle the gods could be. They had smiled on him once, then turned away. Now he could only endure their cold caprices. Resignation froze his face.

Poor man, I thought again. *He needs reassurance*. Before revealing myself, I raised my golden staff,

Caduceus. It was a fine tool, with many powers: it could induce sleep, encourage obedience, and erase memories. Now, waving it once, I cast a spell over the Greek encampment. As quick as thought, every soldier, sheep, horse, chicken, louse, and flea was fast asleep.

How wonderfully easy, I thought, pleased. *I don't do this often enough.*

Then I took off my cap.

Both men froze. Priam released a long, shuddering breath when he recognized me. "Hermes?" he asked.

"Yes, King," I said, and he lowered himself to the ground facedown, arms outstretched in supplication. Idaeus quickly dropped beside him, his broad back twitching with fear.

I told them to rise. Idaeus was on his feet with his head bowed before Priam had struggled to his knees. Seeing that he needed help, I pulled him up, grasping both his bony elbows. The flesh of his arms was as soft and wrinkled as an old wineskin.

"You've come to guide us?" His voice quavered a little.

"As promised," I said, and at this he shook his head repeatedly, as if making a point in conversation with himself. Then he looked up at me with abject gratitude.

"You'll be safe," I told him. "I've made sure of that. Look." I pointed with my staff. Nothing whatsoever moved in the encampment; it was as still as one of the temple friezes at Delphi, and—in my opinion—an even more impressive sight. "They're asleep," I said with satisfaction.

Idaeus made a guttural noise of amazement.

I took up the reins of Priam's war chariot. "I'll drive you in," I said. "Climb on. Idaeus will follow."

Priam hesitated. Then he said, "Tell me, please, Lord Hermes . . ." He faltered and began again. "Is he . . . is Hector—?" He couldn't finish. But I knew the terrible question he was trying to ask. Had Achilles made good his threat? Had he thrown Hector's body to the dogs?

I set his mind at ease. "His body is unharmed. Perfect. Without blemish. The gods have protected it for you."

He nodded rapidly, turning his face away. Idaeus let out a groan of relief.

When they were ready, I led them down to Achilles' tent.

TWENTY-NINE

Achilles accepted Priam's ransom and relinquished Hector, granting the Trojans eleven days to bury him. During that time, he decreed, the war would stop. So the old king brought his son home, and funeral preparations began. The Trojans cut down trees, consecrated the grave site—it was just outside the walls—and set to building the pyre. When the tall wooden platform was ready, they would assemble for the long, solemn rites. Once Hector's bones were collected from the ashes and laid to rest, the truce would end.

Before it did, I paid a call on Apollo. He was exactly where I thought he'd be, in one of his forest camps below the Mount Olympus tree line. It was his favorite, very well hidden.

I found him lolling under a pine, polishing his silver bow, looking relaxed and fit. He jumped to his feet when I appeared. "Wayfinder! You found me!" he joked.

"Took me all day," I claimed, to which he replied, "Ha."

After he'd shown me his favorite hound's new litter, five plump, grublike things with tiny, restless tails, I asked him about the dream he'd sent to Zeus.

"The truth is, I didn't send one," he said, picking up his bow again and rubbing the silver steadily.

"What? Why not?"

"Didn't have to. He changed his mind on his own." He glanced at me. "Between us, I think he's tiring of the war. I know he's tired of fighting with Hera about it. The rest of us aren't getting along, either," he added. "Artemis almost shot Ares the other day because he was saying such hateful things about the Trojans."

She would have hit him, too, I thought. Apollo's twin was the best archer on Olympus.

"Only Ares and Eris watch the fighting anymore. The rest of us are sick of it."

I felt a rush of joy. If I'd been alone, I would have jumped into the air and done a somersault, the way I used to when I first got my sandals. But I maintained my dignity. "I'm happy to hear that," I said.

"Somehow I knew you would be." He smiled. Then he asked, "What happened between Priam and Achilles? You did listen in, didn't you?" Apollo knew about my penchant for eavesdropping. He didn't approve, but he didn't exactly disapprove, either. He almost never pressed me for gossip. I admired his forbearance—secretly, of course.

"Priam went right into the tent," I said. "He knelt before Achilles, weeping. Then he grabbed Achilles' hand and started kissing it."

"The hand that killed his son." Apollo's eyebrows went up a hair.

"Yes. Then Achilles broke down, too, and they both cried and cried. They were alone in his tent in the dead of night—nobody saw."

"Nobody would have believed it."

I nodded. "Finally they stopped, and for a while they just looked at each other, like old friends who knew they'd never meet again. Then Achilles gave Priam the body."

"He really kissed Achilles' hand?" Apollo had never understood my affection for mortals. But from his voice, I knew that my account had moved him.

"One of the saddest things I've ever seen."

"And you've seen a lot." It was almost a question.

I shrugged, not wanting to complain to him. "Lots of dead, anyway. I'm Hermes Infernal now."

He looked at his gleaming silver bow, a weapon that

had killed hundreds of men, and sighed. “It will end soon, brother,” he said. “Take my word for it.”

“Really?”

“In no time they’ll be calling you Luck Bringer again.” It was my favorite title, and sadly out of use these days.

I got to my feet. “Thank you. For everything.”

“Least I could do,” he said.

The eleven days of peace flew by. Hector’s rites were performed with great ceremony before the people of Troy. Then his bones were laid to rest in a royal burial mound to the east of the palace and the Trojans retreated behind the city walls. The Greeks, who had grown increasingly restless, got ready to attack. More violence and suffering were on their way.

Before leaving Olympus and returning to my infernal post, I went to bid farewell to Zeus. He was on the western parapet, gazing down at the earth.

"Father," I said, startling him. "I've come to say goodbye."

"You're going? Why? You just got here!"

"The war starts again tomorrow. I have to guide the dead. Hector is probably waiting for me already."

"Ah," he said, "of course. My son the Psychopomp." Once I'd liked to hear him say it. Now I didn't even smile. *What a stupid title!* I thought. *And I actually used to be proud of it.*

"You seem tired, son," he said. "And we've hardly talked. Come sit with me for a while, won't you?" He settled into his favorite chair, patting the one beside it invitingly.

I sat.

He leaned toward me the way he did when he was about to confide something. "I've been meaning to tell you," he said, "that you did a very good job with Priam. He's been greatly comforted since you helped him."

"And tomorrow, when he loses another son or two," I retorted, "will he be comforted then?" The harsh words hung in the air, surprising us both. I'd never spoken to Zeus this way.

His head went back slightly and his eyes narrowed. But there was no anger in his voice. "Well. Well," he said. "Probably not. But it's war, son. People suffer and die. You have to accept that."

"I can't."

"But—"

I stood. "It's time for me to go."

He, too, got to his feet. "Hermes, you've changed so much! You used to make me laugh all the time, and now you can't even smile. What's happened to you? I'm worried."

In the past I would have welcomed his concern, even basked in it. Now it seemed to me that he was feigning ignorance, and I was disappointed with him.

You know what's happened to me, I thought. *I've been in exile in Hell, hiding out from a war you encouraged. I've been miserably unhappy, not that you noticed, and now you're chiding me because I'm not amusing you.*

"I'll be fine, Father," I said evenly. "Just give me your blessing."

He took my head between his hands, his palms warm on my temples, and I closed my eyes. As he chanted, I saw people, hundreds of them, rebuilding a smoldering, ruined city. It was Troy.

The vision eased my heart a little, and when the blessing was complete and Zeus' big, solid hands were resting on my shoulders, I could look at him without rancor.

"I'll be back when the war ends," I said.

And then I left him.

PART FIVE

The Ocean's Navel

THIRTY

I kept my word to Zeus. When the war ended and the dead no longer thronged to Hades, I returned to Olympus.

Now that the gods had stopped conniving, it was a far more tranquil place. Hera and Zeus renewed their marriage vows. Aphrodite gave Athena a tall jar of wrinkle-reducing face cream, and they buried the hatchet. Ares, despondent without his daily battles, retreated to his armory. Eris went away somewhere to sulk.

I recovered slowly. Playing my pipes helped, and so did dancing with the Graces, but nothing cheered me as much as reclaiming Pegasus. The dryads had cared for him in my absence, and, as forest spirits will, they'd adorned him with vines and wildflowers, tufts of moss, and a garland of bright red berries. None of it diminished his beauty.

On the day I came for him, he greeted me with a long, throaty, almost reproachful nicker. As we left the forest, I stroked his neck and told him he looked silly. Then we took to the heavens.

We wandered for days. I sang many songs to him about how much I'd missed him, and when I stopped, so had the hateful whispering in my head.

Some days later, on a sunny spring afternoon, Zeus summoned me. Finding the audience hall empty—it often was at this hour—I went out to the western terrace. Zeus had recently taken up gardening. Now he was on his knees, pruning an enormous climbing rose. After sending a vague gesture of greeting in my direction, he resumed his work, studying the thorny green branch before him as if it contained a hidden message. Then he made his cut, studied the branch again, and moved on to the next. His deep, tuneless humming was like the song of a giant bee.

I was perfectly content to idle in the garden, but after he'd pruned dozens of branches without saying a word or looking my way, I decided he'd forgotten me. At that very moment he said, "You seem happier these days."

I told him I was.

"What would make you happier still?"

The question surprised me. Zeus often wanted to know what I thought, but only if I could help him solve a problem. Otherwise, he tended to command.

I phrased my answer carefully. "Not that I'm complaining," I said, "but I'd rather bring luck to the living than comfort to the dead."

"Hmm." He got to his feet, wiped his hands on his robe, then drank thirstily from a silver goblet. His wide brow was sweaty and streaked with dirt, but it was smooth again; the deep lines and furrows of the war years had gone. He, too, was happier these days.

"I think I have the perfect mission for you," he said. "Have you ever heard of the Ocean's Navel?"

When I shook my head, he sank into a chair and motioned for me to join him.

"It's an island called Ogygia," he said, "in the very center of the ocean, which is how it got its nickname. The nymph Calypso lives there, with Odysseus."

"The Greek captain?" Odysseus had planned, designed, and helped to build the Trojan Horse, a brilliant hoax that led directly to Troy's downfall. I'd been curious about him for years. I've always liked wily mortals.

"The very same," said Zeus. "He and his men were shipwrecked on their way home from Troy. Odysseus was the only survivor, because Calypso rescued him."

"And he stayed with her?"

"She's been keeping him there for years."

"Keeping him? How?"

"Spells, good food, stunning physical beauty."

None of that sounded half bad to me. "And the problem is . . . ?" I asked.

"The problem is, he's miserable. He yearns for his wife and son and for his homeland, Ithaca. Athena and Hera have been badgering me to help him, so I finally said I would."

Aha, I thought.

"Somebody's got to talk to Calypso," he continued, "persuade her to let him go. I know you have a lot to do . . ."

Not exactly, I thought.

". . . but I was thinking you might be interested."

I faked a frown. "Let me make sure I understand you, Father. You're asking me to visit a beautiful nymph on her own private island and bend her to my will?"

"Exactly. What do you say?"

I told him I would try to find the time.

So here I was, skimming across the vast ocean at dawn with a school of dolphins for company, hoping to catch a glimpse of Ogygia. Zeus had warned me that it was tiny, so every now and then I rose high into the air to get a bird's-eye view. When I saw a perfectly round island and the lone man on its western beach looking out to sea, I knew I had reached my destination.

THIRTY-ONE

"You like to make men cry?" The moment I said it, Calypso flinched, and I cringed. We were in her cavern, a tall, rocky alcove where cooing seabirds nested in the upper ledges, and so far I had made nothing but mistakes.

I had barely stepped inside before blurting out Zeus' decree. I had accepted her hospitality—nectar in shell cups, served at a pink coral table—with a gawky nod. Beneath her filmy gown, which changed from blue to green when she moved, her skin was pearly, her body sinuous. It was hard not to stare, so I stared.

And now I was insulting her. *Shouldn't drink in the morning,* I told myself, eyeing the translucent webbing between her fingers, the delicate filigree of scales around her wrists and ankles. They shone like silver.

Her eyes shone, too—with indignation.

"Of course not," she said. "I love him. I want to make him happy!"

"Happy?" I echoed. "He's out on the beach weeping, and the sun's barely up! He's miserable!" I'd gotten a good look at Odysseus on my way in. With his big shoulders hunched and tears sliding into his unkempt, grizzled beard, he was the picture of woe.

I saw that I had wounded Calypso again. She peered into her cup as if she might find consolation there, and her lovely mouth quivered. I waited, thinking she might reply, but she said nothing. In that brief silence I was able to muster my wits.

"Let him go, Calypso," I said. "Zeus wishes it, and he himself sent me here to tell you. Obey him—you know you must."

Her head dipped, acknowledging this, and I went

on: "Besides, it's the only way you'll ever make Odysseus happy. Give him what he wants."

She drained her cup. "I can't bear to lose him," she confessed. In an effort to stave off her tears, she swallowed, shook her head, and looked down again, but the tears came anyway.

I thought of the dead, their lives cut short, and of old Priam, kneeling before Achilles. *So much grief*, I thought. *And now here's more*. I sighed, wondering if I could do anything to console her. "I know about loss, how painful it can be," I said. "I'm sorry for yours."

"Are you?" It was a whisper of resignation, hardly more than a sigh. I had the impulse to fold her in my arms and kiss her salty cheek. It wasn't the nectar, either; my pity for her came directly from my sober heart.

"You'll recover. In time."

She collected herself, wiping her shining eyes,

then clearing her throat. She blew her nose daintily on the hem of her gown before standing.

"You know," I said, indicating my staff, Caduceus, "I can make you forget. After he goes, I mean." Along with its other powers—inducing sleep, encouraging obedience, scratching an itchy back—Caduceus could erase bad memories. "Less pain that way," I added.

She gleamed, even in the dim light of the cavern. "No," she said. "I don't want to forget."

I'll admit it: I was jealous of Odysseus for winning such love from her. And her resolve moved me. "I respect that," I managed to say, while my heart flopped like a fish on a line.

She rewarded me with a fleeting smile. Then she walked outside to join Odysseus.

Why did I stay? Part of it was diligence. Hard worker that I am, I wanted to make sure that Calypso obeyed

Zeus' command. The rest was curiosity. How would Calypso tell Odysseus he was free to go, if indeed she told him? Would she mention me? What would she say? I had to know.

So, after taking to the air as if I were leaving, I donned my cap, wheeled around, and landed on the beach like an oversized gull, a stone's throw from Odysseus.

He was exactly where I'd left him, on his haunches facing the ocean. Now that the sky was brighter, his weeping eyes were shut against the light, so he didn't see Calypso when she approached. Or perhaps he didn't want to.

She had to touch his shoulder before he looked up at her. "I have something to tell you," she said. "I've kept you here long enough. I've decided to let you go."

He froze, head cocked. "Don't mock me, Calypso," he said gruffly.

"I'm not."

"How can I believe you?" he demanded. "I've begged and pleaded and wept like a child for years, yet you kept me here. And now, just like that"—he snapped his fingers—"you've changed your mind?" He shook his head. "You're lying."

"I'll take an oath."

He stood. He was a big man, solid and sun-darkened, his broad chest streaked with rosy battle scars. "Take it, then," he said, folding his arms.

Calypso swore a ringing oath—by the earth, the sky, and the swirling waters of the River Styx—that she would help Odysseus leave. Standing tall, every lustrous inch of her a reproach to his ingratitude, she added, "May the gods strike me dead if I harbor even a single thought of bringing you back."

We waited. Wave after wave rushed in and sped away. A crab tiptoed over my invisible foot. Calypso stayed alive.

"Oof, I'm sorry," said Odysseus. His head dipped apologetically. "Forgive my harsh words?"

"I'll try," said Calypso. "Meanwhile, let's build you a raft."

THIRTY-TWO

After much hard work, Odysseus was ready for his journey. He had a wide, seaworthy raft, its sails woven by Calypso herself. He had a generous supply of food, water, and wine. He had a silver knife and a bronze ax. And now that he was bathed and dressed in clean robes, he had the look of a king again, too.

"I'm grateful to you, Calypso," he called from the shallows. "I'll never forget you."

"Nor I you," she replied. Then she lifted her arms above her head and whirled, invoking the wind with her long braids flying. It came at once. Before she had spun around three times, a mighty gust had filled Odysseus' sails and borne him out to sea.

Calypso stood there until the raft was only a bobbing speck. Then she dropped to the sand and fell onto her back, arms and legs outspread, hands open wide. She lay there, looking up at the sky. "I'm alone," she whispered.

No, you're not, I thought. I hovered above her, glad for the chance to admire her fully, yet sorry for her grief, which came off her in waves, like heat.

Before I left, I brushed her hand with my staff, as lightly as a sand flea, banishing her memories of Odysseus.

Just in case I decided to come back.

Of course I went back. I couldn't keep away. And I am happy to say that my second visit to Calypso was much better than the first. I had no unpleasant directives this time, and Odysseus was gone and forgotten, which helped. When she welcomed me warmly, I responded in kind.

"You're looking lovelier than ever," I blurted, thinking how much easier it was to speak on Zeus' behalf than on my own. Yet for some reason my awkwardness didn't put her off. She invited me to stay, and I did.

Calypso and I spent our time together in wondrous ways. She took me far beneath the sea to meet her Oceanid sisters and Nereid cousins. We traveled to the hidden coves of the Cyclades, where Poseidon's wife, Amphitrite, farms her fabled pearls. We listened to Sirens. We listened to whales. And we visited Aegae, Poseidon's home, to pay our respects to the Lord of the Oceans himself.

I hadn't seen my uncle for so long that I'd forgotten how imposing he was, with his blue hair and beard, his broad chest, and his extraordinary deep voice, like the rumblings of a distant earthquake. But I'd remembered him as genial, and indeed he was.

After many wet embraces and hearty claps on the back, he insisted on taking us on a personal tour of his stables, saying he'd heard I liked horses.

I admitted that I did, marveling at the sight of his hundred white stallions in their immaculate stalls. Their manes and tails were the color of sea foam, their eyes dark coral red. While Calypso walked down the center aisle, caressing their noses one by one, Poseidon said, "I hear you've tamed Pegasus."

It was odd that he knew, I thought. "I ride him when I can."

"Beautiful creature." He said the words with such pride that I stared at him. In return he lifted an eyebrow, looking smug, and I wondered what he was actually letting me know. I'd often speculated about Pegasus; his sudden appearance after Medusa's death was a puzzle I'd never been able to solve. How did it happen? Who was responsible? It was as if he'd been conjured up by another Immortal, but that was unlikely—nobody played such outlandish tricks but me. In all my musings, I'd never dreamed the winged horse might be Poseidon's offspring. Yet that was what my uncle seemed to be hinting.

"Yours?" I asked.

He nodded.

"With Medusa?" *Now, there's a freakish combination*, I thought as Poseidon held a finger to his lips, enjoining my silence.

At last I knew why I liked Pegasus so much. We were cousins.

Calypso had never been above the earth, much less to Olympus. She asked about it often, plying me with endless questions about life atop the mountain. How did the Immortals dress? What were their dwellings like? Did they keep pets? What did they do for amusement? Would I take her up there sometime?

"Of course."

"When?" she asked eagerly.

Before I knew it, I'd agreed to visit Olympus in two days' time. While Calypso conjured up a shimmering new gown for the journey and did elaborate things with her hair, I made a few preparations of my own.

We set off early on a fine, bright, cloudless morning. Calypso kept her arms loosely folded around my neck so that I could pull her along, and we made a smooth ascent at a moderate pace. When we were aloft, I moved more quickly, going from tortoise-racing-hare to hare-fleeing-fox. We hardly spoke as we flew east over the glinting turquoise of the ocean, though Calypso murmured with delight many times, and when she saw our destination, she gasped. It rose out of the plains like a stone giant, its massive, snowy head so fiercely white that it discouraged direct scrutiny.

"There it is," I said. "Olympus."

"Ah!" She squeezed me and kissed my neck. "This is going to be wonderful!"

That depends, I thought, *on my fellow Olympians*.

THIRTY-THREE

I'd always known I'd have to be careful if Calypso and I ever visited Olympus together. The reason was simple: I'd never told her how I'd erased her memories of Odysseus. *Much better that she doesn't know*, I'd often thought. *Why should she? It would only cause her distress.* But deep down I knew the real reason I kept it a secret: I was afraid she'd hate me if she found out.

So before our excursion I'd made a few lists:

Olympians to Visit

Apollo (if he's around; she'll love his dogs)

Artemis (ditto, though probably hunting)

Aphrodite (Calypso admires her; thinks they're cousins)

Hephaestus (she'll like his workshop)

Olympians to Avoid

Ares (Lord of Unpleasantness;
always first on the Avoid list)
Hera (may hold a grudge against
Calypso because of Odysseus)
Athena (see above, but worse)

My plan was to keep Calypso away from anybody who might refer to Odysseus. I was reasonably sure that Apollo, Artemis, and Aphrodite wouldn't, because they'd been allied with the Trojans. Hephaestus, like Demeter, had stayed fairly neutral, so he wasn't a worry.

I was undecided about Zeus, but as it happened, he was away when we arrived, attending a World Religions conference in Babylon. Even better, Hera had gone with him.

Otherwise, we kept to my hidden agenda. We stayed far from Ares' armory and skirted the field Athena used for lance practice. We dropped in on Hephaestus, artisan of the gods, who showed us some of his recent inventions: a puffy silken tunic padded with goose feathers; a four-pronged silver tool with a very long handle for placing and turning meat offerings on a fire; an arrangement of long, thin golden tubes strung on wire that chimed sweetly in the wind; and an odd contraption made of fine bronze mesh and leather straps, meant to gird the breast.

"It's a protective undergarment for women," Hephaestus explained. "I'm not sure how comfortable it is, but Athena said she'd try it out the next time she goes into battle."

Knowing he took his creative efforts seriously, I bade him a hasty farewell and pulled Calypso out of his workshop before she burst into incredulous laughter. She was still giggling about protective undergarments when we found Apollo and Artemis at the edge of the Western Forest. The sight of the twins, geared up for the hunt and surrounded by a seething pack of wolfhounds, sobered her quickly.

Artemis, virginal Moon Goddess and Mistress of the Wild, is a stern creature who shuns low tricksters like me, preferring the company of her furiously devoted and very chaste young nymphs. I'd never been able to make her laugh, though I'd tried everything from centaur jokes to silly faces. So it didn't surprise me that now, after a single glance at Calypso's ornate braids and sheer, clinging gown, she greeted us with reserve.

Apollo made up for her lack of warmth, though. He suggested rather briskly that Artemis start off without him, which she did. Then he embraced us and introduced Calypso to every single one of his hounds. Amber eyes aglow, they licked her hand eagerly when she offered it.

"So sweet!" she cooed, enjoying their affection. Apollo and I shared a smile, having seen these very hounds bring down their prey swiftly and ruthlessly, only to come up for air grinning, their faces besmeared with blood.

"Very sweet," I said, "and very well disciplined. Just like their master."

"Ho," Apollo retorted dryly, before asking how long we'd be staying on Olympus.

"Not much longer," I said. "We'll say hello to Aphrodite, then head for home."

"Home?" The deep blue eyes widened very slightly. Officially my home was on Olympus. "Well, well."

I reached for Calypso's hand. "It's a fine little island," I said. "Very peaceful."

"I wish you happiness there." He placed a hand on my shoulder, patting it. I covered his hand with mine, and we said our farewells.

THIRTY-FOUR

Calypso had always been eager to meet Aphrodite. She was certain that the Love Goddess, born out of the sea, must be a relation, albeit a distant one. As we approached the goddess's sanctuary, I teased, "Looking forward to meeting your long-lost cousin?"

"I am," she replied. "You know I admire her."

And you certainly share some of her powers, I thought. *Keeping Odysseus for seven years was no mean feat*. "I'm sure she'll admire you, too," I said.

"Flatterer." She kissed me.

By this time we were standing beneath one of the wild fig trees bordering Aphrodite's woodland retreat. She called the place the Grove of Eternal Beauty; I'd never dared to ask if the beauty was hers or the grove's.

Calypso certainly found the grove beautiful, exclaiming over every one of its features—the pools with their lazy orange fish, the long rows of cherry trees in radiant bloom, the silky grass, even the fragrance of the air, which grew stronger as we neared Aphrodite's marble pavilion.

And there we found her, supine on a pillow-strewn platform. Two little satyrs were fanning her with white peacock feathers while a pair of nymphs tended to her fingernails and a third nymph massaged her feet. Yet another nymph was removing the linen cloth covering her brow when we appeared. Seeing us, she sat up with a languid smile.

"Hermes! What brings you here? And who is your lovely companion?" Eyes bright with interest, she extended a delicate white hand to Calypso, who dropped to one knee before taking it.

"This is Calypso," I said, "of the island Ogygia."

"Ogygia?" she repeated. "I know I've heard that name. Was it from Zeus?" she wondered aloud.

Oh, no! I thought. Panic reached into my throat and squeezed it hard. Had Zeus told Aphrodite about my mission to free Odysseus?

I made some choking noises, which Aphrodite waved away.

"It's called something else, too, isn't it? No, no, don't tell me!" She raised an admonitory finger while she searched her memory. "I know! The Ocean's Navel!"

Calypso, who was still kneeling with her head bowed, nodded.

Wondering what Aphrodite knew, I caught her eyes with my own. *Mercy, Goddess!* I beseeched silently. She gave me a sly smile and then tugged at Calypso's hand. "Get up, get up, please, my dear," she urged. "Sit here beside me." She patted a cushion invitingly. "I want to hear all about you and Hermes. He's been staying with you on your little island, has he?" When Calypso murmured that I was, Aphrodite's sea-green eyes glinted with mischief. "You must have enchanted him!" she exclaimed.

I'm ruined! I thought. Then, coward that I am, I fled.

It took every scrap of willpower I had to return, but return I did, prepared to face the worst. Yet the worst never came. When I reappeared, Aphrodite chided me for running off so quickly, and Calypso smiled at me with her usual affection. She looked splendid, and I told her so.

"Aphrodite shared some of her face and body creams with me," she said. "And look what her nymphs did!" She held out her hands so I could admire her scarlet fingernails.

"Like rose-fingered Dawn," I said. "Very pretty." I turned to Aphrodite. "Thank you for your generosity, Goddess."

"Yes, thank you for everything!" Calypso began to

kneel, but Aphrodite stopped her. "Cousin, it was my pleasure. Come back whenever you like."

Speechless with joy, Calypso grasped my hand.

Aphrodite smiled at us sweetly. "Bless you both," she said. "Hermes, take good care of her."

Grateful for Aphrodite's discretion, I vowed fervently that I would, and I did. In time the secret of how I'd used Caduceus to win Calypso ceased to gnaw at me, replaced by the conviction that I, Luck Bringer, had finally found luck.

Our love deepened, and we had many fine children.

No spells or magical devices were used.

They weren't necessary.

MOUNT OLYMPUS
TROY
THESSALY
GULF OF CORINTH
ARCADIA
ARGOS
SERIPHOS
OGYGIA
IONIAN SEA
CRETE
SEA OF CYRENE

ANCIENT GREECE
CIRCA 1500 B.C.
CYPRUS
TERRANEAN
SEA
JOPPA

GLOSSARY OF CHARACTERS

Gods and Mythical Creatures

Aphrodite (af-roh-dy-tee): The beautiful, seductive Goddess of Love, a daughter of Zeus, was the wife of Hephaestus and the mother of Eros.

Apollo (a-pol-lo): The God of Prophecy, also a healer. Apollo's temple at Delphi, with its many snake-wielding oracles, was renowned throughout the ancient world.

Ares (air-eez): The God of War.

Argos: A hundred-eyed monster.

Artemis (ahr-tuh-mis): The Goddess of the Hunt, the Moon Goddess, and Apollo's virginal twin sister.

Athena (a-thee-na): The Goddess of Wisdom. Athena sprang fully grown out of Zeus' head, causing the first known splitting headache in mythological history.

Calypso (ka-lip-so): A sea nymph and enchantress.

Cerberus (sur-bur-us): The three-headed watchdog of the Underworld.

Charon (kair-un): The ferryman who rowed the dead across the River Styx.

Demeter (dih-mee-tur): The Goddess of the Harvest and Fertility and the mother of Kore.

Dryads (dry-ads): Forest and tree spirits.

Eris (ee-ris): Ares' sister; also called Spite and Discord.

Eros (air-ohs): Aphrodite's mischievous young son. Eros spent his time shooting magical golden arrows at mortals. His targets fell hopelessly in love.

Furies: Three crone-like sisters who pursued and tormented erring mortals; also called Erinyes (ih-rin-ee-eez).

Hades (hay-deez): Brother of Zeus and Poseidon and the God of the Underworld.

Hephaestus (huh-fes-tus): The God of Fire and a master

artisan. His creations included magical armor, self-propelled tripods, and mechanical golden servants.

Hera (hair-uh): The Goddess of Marriage and Zeus' wife.

Hermes (hur-meez): Zeus' personal messenger. Hermes also brought luck, protected travelers, escorted the dead, invented musical instruments, played pranks, and stole.

Hestia (hes-tee-uh): The Goddess of the Hearth.

Hymenaeus (hy-mun-ee-us): The God of Marriage.

Iris (eye-ris): The Goddess of Rainbows.

Kore (kohr-ee): Demeter's daughter; called Persephone after her marriage to Hades.

Medusa (muh-doo-suh): A young woman turned into a snake-haired monster by Athena; sometimes called a Gorgon.

Nereids (nee-ree-ids): The fifty nymphs of the calm sea, daughters of the old ocean god Nereus and the Oceanid Doris.

Oceanids (oh-see-uh-nids): The 3,000 sea nymphs born to the river god Oceanus and his consort Tethys.

Oenone (eh-noh-nee): A nymph of Mount Ida in love with Paris.

Pegasus (peg-uh-sus): A winged horse who sprang out of Medusa's headless body.

Persephone (pur-sef-ih-nee): Demeter's daughter. Kore became known as Persephone after marrying Hades.

Poseidon (puh-sy-dun): Lord of the Oceans and brother of Zeus and Hades; also called Earth Shaker for his power to cause earthquakes.

Tityus (tit-ee-us): A giant, son of Zeus and the Earth Goddess, Gaia.

Zeus (zoos): Most powerful of all the gods, Zeus had many appellations, including Lord of the Universe, Deliverer, Cloud Gatherer, and Averter of Flies.

Mortals

Achilles (uh-kil-eez): Greatest of the Greek warriors in the Trojan War.

Acrisius (uh-kree-zhus): Danae's father; King of Argos.

Agenor (ag-uh-nor): Andromeda's betrothed.

Andromeda (an-drahm-ih-duh): Daughter of the King and Queen of Joppa, she wed Perseus after he rescued her.

Ascalaphus (as-kal-uh-fus): Hades' gardener.

Atalanta (at-uh-lan-tuh): An Arcadian princess, known as the swiftest mortal in the world.

Cassiope (kuh-sy-uh-pee): Andromeda's mother.

Cepheus (see-fee-us): Andromeda's father.

Danae (dan-ay-ee): Perseus' mother.

Dictys (dik-tis): A fisherman on the island of Seriphos.

Helen: A great beauty, married to King Menelaus of Sparta.

Idaeus (ih-day-us): King Priam's servant.

Menelaus (men-uh-lay-us): With his brother, Agamemnon, he led the Greek forces in the war against Troy.

Molpus: A blind singer.

Odysseus (oh-dis-ee-us): The Greek captain whose ten-year journey home after the Trojan War is described in Homer's epic poem *The Odyssey*.

Pandora: The first woman, fashioned out of clay by Hephaestus and sent to earth by Zeus to release misery into the world.

Paris: The prince of Troy whose seduction of Helen led to the Trojan War.

Peleus (peh-lay-us): Achilles' father.

Perseus (pur-see-us): The Greek hero who beheaded Medusa and then used her head as a weapon to vanquish his foes.

Polydectes (pahl-ee-dek-teez): King of Seriphos and

Danae's suitor.

Priam (pry-em): King of Troy.

Sisyphus (sis-ih-fus): King and founder of the city of Corinth; doomed to eternal torment for defying Zeus.

Tantalus (tan-tuh-lus): Punished with constant, gnawing hunger for offering the gods a meal of human flesh.

AUTHOR'S NOTE

I set out to write about Hermes because he had a unique position in the Greek pantheon. He was the only Immortal familiar with the three worlds of gods, mortals, and shades, and he was Zeus' personal messenger as well as his son and confidant. In addition, he was gifted with speed, flight, invisibility, and prophecy. If he was never the central figure in the myths in which he appeared, he sometimes played an important part in them, and he always knew more about them than any of the other characters. Add to this his cunning, his curiosity, and his mischievous nature, and you get Hermes, the ultimate Olympian insider.

But there was more to him than his access to privileged information. There was his geniality, which never seemed to sour; his deep love of music; and his affection for animals. He was impressively versatile, too: he guided shepherds, conferred fertility and prosperity, invented musical instruments, and led the nymphs and the Graces in dance. He was also a master of knots and chains, which no doubt helped him in his thievery.

Hermes liked mischief but not cruelty, and was more reliably kind to mortals than the other gods. For this he was well loved. The thousands of pillars called *herms*, erected to him throughout ancient Greece, attest to his popularity, as does the fact that at a certain point in his career, he became a protector of children and the god of education.

My affection for Hermes grew when I learned that he hated violence. It made me certain that I wanted to write *Quicksilver* and helped to shape the book. Thinking about this aspect of his personality gave me the order of events and their emotional tone and colored the way I imagined many of the other characters.

As for *what* I imagined and what I didn't, readers of Greek mythology probably know the myth in which the infant Hermes steals Apollo's cattle—it's the only one in which he takes center stage. They may have noticed him in all the many versions of the myth of Demeter and Kore/Persephone, the myth of Perseus and Medusa, and the myth called the Judgment of Paris, where his role is much smaller. Mythology zealots will also know the myth about Zeus and Io, in which Hermes kills Argos at Zeus' command.

I based two episodes of *Quicksilver* on Homer: Priam's visit to Achilles' tent in *The Iliad* and Calypso's release of Odysseus in *The Odyssey*. Needless to say, anyone with an interest in Greek mythology should read Homer's epic masterpieces.

Hermes was a prankster, but examples of his humor are hard to find. I was forced to invent his jokes, and I apologize for them. Other events in *Quicksilver*, and Hermes' many changes of heart, are my invention, too.

STEPHANIE SPINNER's books for young readers include *Quiver*, which *Booklist* called a "stirring novel" in a starred review, *Aliens for Breakfast* and *Aliens for Lunch* (both with Jonathan Etra), and *Aliens for Dinner*.

Stephanie Spinner lives in Sherman, Connecticut.